Brazen

Scarlett Redd

Published by Scarlett Redd, 2024.

BRAZEN

First edition. March 22, 2024.

Copyright © 2024 Scarlett Redd.

ISBN: 979-8224436446

Written by Scarlett Redd.

Brazen
By
Scarlett Redd

Please Note: There may be some triggers for people in this book. There is some violence, sexual assault, and other life events, including loss. I want to thank my readers who gave me a chance and read my work. Thank you to Christian Ares for putting up with me and helping me when I needed it with all your poking, prodding, and encouragement along the way to keep me going and hit publish once again. I'm glad I have such a great friend, and I can't thank you enough for all you do to help and encourage me. I want to thank my Cover Model, Phil Bruce, for his patience with the delays I've had along the way. I'd also like to thank Tracie Soxie Weston of Soxsational Cover Art for another fantastic cover. I'd also like to thank my family and friends, who encourage me & keep me going. Scarlett

Chapter One – Brazen

I woke with a start and groaned, stretching my body out before I tried to get out of bed. Right now, that the hard part was done, I was ready to prepare for another day ahead. I got up and began walking down the hallway to the kitchen. Once there, I prepared to make myself an espresso coffee, needing my morning kick-start to the day. Unfortunately, it was a cold and frosty morning outside; therefore, it was very much needed. Once my cup of coffee had been processed through the coffee machine, I took my cup out onto the rear patio, shivering in the cold. I don't know what I was thinking. I was still in my boxer shorts and a t-shirt and started getting goosebumps and blue balls.

I placed my cup on the table while picking up my cigarette packet from the pot in the middle. I shook one out, put it in my mouth, and grabbed my lighter. I rolled the wheel and lit my cigarette, taking a big puff. I should give up this filthy habit. Well, maybe another day, but today was not that day. "Aah," nothing like that first drag for the day. I released my breath, watching the smoke swirl into the chilly air. I watched, mesmerized, watching my cigarette smoke rise. Then, I watched as it dispersed, mixing in with the cold morning air.

I was Brazen by name and Brazen by nature. I'm the Prez of my sector from the Texas Mafia. I put my foot on one of the chairs around the table, resting my elbow on my knee. I had been lucky in life. At the same time, I glanced around and surveyed everything I fortunately owned. I'm too fortunate for my luck some days. One day, it would all go pear-shaped; of that, there was no doubt. I felt it in my gut. I had a two-story hacienda with six bedrooms and nine bathrooms. Who the fuck needs more bathrooms than bedrooms? But, hey, it is what it is. I also had about four small cottages scattered about the yard to take any overflow when my men stayed over, and I didn't have enough spare rooms in the house. Out the back, from the veranda, I overlooked a swimming pool and spa. In the distance, a view of the Carolina sapphire trees for privacy. They have a dual use, hiding the six-foot-high stone wall surrounding my property. I needed many hidden security cameras to secure my 7.7k square foot lot.

Today, I was meeting up with a few of our other brother members. They needed help with a dispute with some members of their enemy factions. These assholes, were causing them grief with the products they were shipping? Although we usually worked alone, we sometimes needed backup for projects. This was one of those times when we were helping other fraternity members. I hoped everything would run smoothly without any problems. We didn't need to run into any trouble on our mission. We needed to help bring down the Mexican mafia trying to muscle in on our turf.

We needed to show them they had run afoul of us in their pursuits. I was more careful and tried to keep my nose clean in my dealings. It had led me to stay out of trouble so far anyway. But even I know something is coming. I'm not stupid enough in this life. Something might happen one day, although I always hope it never will.

Molotov, my offsider, or Mo for short. He helped with security and any other problems that needed disposal. Please don't ask me how he got his name, but I'm sure there's a clue somewhere in his name. He was my sidekick, always there without fail. He nodded in my direction when he also headed out with his coffee in hand.

I lifted my chin in response. He was a man of few words. Then, after blowing out a puff of smoke. I greeted him. "Morning, what's up, Mo?"

"Morning. I'm here giving the heads up that we have another problem."

"Oh! Christ, what now? Dare I ask?" I raised my eyebrows in his direction.

"There might be some trafficked women at the destination tonight," I informed Brazen after blowing out a puff of smoke and taking a sip of my coffee.

"Oh fuck. That's all we need. Let's add another problem to the already terrible equation. We better take extra backup with us tonight. Just in case we need help getting the women out, too." *I may not lead a divine life, but I draw the line at human trafficking.* "I'm glad you found that extra fucking information out. It saved us from any major surprises or problems we might encounter tonight. No way could we have got them all out on our bikes. Now I know to take a couple of vans with us."

"Yeah. I always have my ears out listening, man. You never know what you might learn, that's for sure. I always blend into the background with my ears open," grinning at Brazen, pleased with myself.

"Yes, you do. I am still determining where I'd be without you at times. Okay, let's round up any extra security men you might need to bring them for backup. We will have the numbers to help us with everything else. I'll come with you and help you find where the women are being held. When we see how many women there are, we decide if we must focus on them over the other problem. I'd rather get them out first. Then I know they're safe from harm before we deal with the other thugs."

"Yep. I will Brazen. I'll get all the weapons. I'll bring my favorite weapon of choice to burn the place down after we're finished," flashing me an evil grin.

"Aah, where would we be without you and your special cocktails? But let's wait and see what happens first before we use that method of attack," I winked at Mo.

"Can you tell the men to be ready for church in the basement at two this afternoon? They need to prepare to discuss our plan of attack and sort out the weapons we will be taking with us?"

"Sure. I'll see you later. I'll go grab a quick nap before then," I yawned.

I grinned at him. "You've been out fucking all night, haven't you? You're such a dirty man whore Mo."

"I will neither confirm nor deny that statement, Boss." He told me while turning around, disappearing inside, and heading toward his room.

I could only shake my head, chuckling at his cheek and ballsy attitude.

Chapter Two – Brazen

Two o'clock came quicker than I expected. I made my way down to the basement with Mo. All our men were there already, judging by the noise of chatter rising from the basement while waiting for us to arrive. When I stepped from the last step, their conversation immediately ceased. Excellent, they knew the protocol when I entered a room. "Men," I nodded, and they raised their chins in response. "Right tonight, we're raiding the Red Belly's warehouse because they took a quantity of the Black Diamond's product, which they are now trying to pass off as their own out on their turf. Recently, Mo discovered some new intel for us. Torres is keeping women of an unknown number and origin imprisoned in his basement. Mo heard earlier that Torres is getting ready to ship them out shortly, so we must rescue them while at his compound.

At the same time, all of you men will be helping the Diamonds sort out the Red Bellies on-site at the warehouse. Mo and I will go to the basement to see what we can find. We will also help the women to safety so they're not in danger from what you're doing upstairs. We should be able to sneak them out of the basement. But if we cannot, Mo or I will guard them. Then, one of us will come back upstairs to help you. When it is safe, we will ship them to safety and shelter when it's all over. Where will that be? I'll decide when we find out the number of women being held there. Also, my decision will determine who can take them. Are we all clear on what's happening tonight?"

"Yes." they all chorused in unison.

"Does anyone else have any questions?"

Arrow, sitting in the back, cocky with bravado, asks me. "What time are we heading off tonight, Prez?"

"Yes, great question, Arrow. It's good to know someone is here to keep me on my toes, which is pleasing. Be ready to leave here at 6 p.m.

sharp. We should arrive at our destination at approximately 7 p.m. Be here at 5.30 with your weapons of choice and anything else you think you will need for the mission. When we've completed our mission, we will meet back here to recap and decide our next action. We need to go over the mission should we need to discuss anything. Right, men, if that's all, you're dismissed. I'll see you all back here at 5.30." I turned and left the basement with Mo following close on my heels. I headed towards my office to check my emails to see if I had any more updates from the Black Diamonds chief, Marcus.

"What do you reckon with those women?" I asked Mo, who had now joined me in my office and sat in the chair opposite my desk. "If there are not too many women, we will return them to my house. I will give them TLC, feed them, and provide shelter tonight, giving me more time to decide where to send them tomorrow. Should there be more women than we can cope with? I'll contact Sherry at the shelter and let her know we have some women rescues for her. I'll give her a hefty donation for the extra trouble of looking after the women I drop on her. Later, when they are ready to leave into Sherry's care, I will give the women some extra money to start themselves elsewhere when they're ready to leave.

"She'll always find room for them; she's an amazing woman. I don't know how she does it, and she's always happy to help us out," he smiled.

"I bet you have a thing for her, don't you?" I raised my eyebrows at him in jest.

"Nope," he was quick to respond.

"You answered that question a bit too fast there, brother. I know you do. I can see it—no need to hide it from me. You two would make a lovely couple. Concentrate on her. Settle down with her and make her your woman. Instead of going around like the man whore you are, if you're not careful, your dick will drop off one day. I know..." I put my hands up in surrender. "I apologize if I sound like your dad. You two work well together. I've seen how happy you two are when you're together. Okay, conversation over..." Judging by the scowl on his face, I could see he wasn't impressed with my observations. This time, no amount of pushing his buttons would make him respond to my line of questioning.

"No ties needed in this life, brother! No one to mourn for me should the worst happen. There is always something bad happening in this lifestyle. It is unfair to be tied to a woman and start a family in this life we lead. I live by my motto, and nothing or no one will change my mind," I glared at Brazen.

"Duly noted," I winked at him, shaking my head and grinning like I knew something he didn't. I stood up from behind my desk. "I'll head off to shower and change for our mission. I'll see you shortly." I patted him on the back of the shoulder in passing.

"Yup," leaning back in his chair with his hands behind his head and his left leg crossed over his right knee. "You better not forget it either, Braze."

Chapter Three - Christa

How had I found myself in this dark, damp basement, chained to a wall? I thought I was alone when I came around, wondering what hell hole I had found myself in. Wherever had I the misfortune to get taken to by those men? Before I knew it, I must have been drugged by someone at the club where I was with my friends. Now, here I was, being held prisoner in this basement. Once my eyes became accustomed to the dark, I noticed I was not alone, and other girls were chained in here besides myself. I had no idea how I had found myself in this mess. I was thankful at least my friends had escaped this misfortune.

I was on holiday with a couple of my girlfriends, touring around Paris. Someone must have drugged my drink in the nightclub we had gone to. I was enjoying a night of fun and dancing the night away. The next thing I knew, I started feeling dizzy and staggering around. I was attempting to find my friends after a visit to the bathroom. Finally, I managed to find an empty table. I collapsed in the seat at an open booth, and everything went black. The next thing I knew, I was waking up in this hell hole.

I'm sure my father must be sick with worry about me. He tended to spoil me. It was how I pretended things were to make myself feel better. It was more like he hated the sight of me. He kept reminding me that I was the spitting image of my mother. I'm sure she was the love of his life, which made him sad when she died from a drug overdose. Whether it was accidental or intentional, I will never know I was too young.

He hadn't dated any other women since she had died. Whether that was his way of coping in his mourning period or that he didn't care about me anymore. Although plenty had tried and flung themselves at him for his wealth, they had all failed. I'm sure he probably took a quick fuck here and there. I wasn't deaf. Depending on where he had spent the night, I would hear him throwing them out in the morning. Or I would listen to the front door open and him trying to sneak quietly up the stairs, but he never did. He was probably still drunk when he staggered up the stairs. On other mornings, after hearing voices arguing, I would hear his bedroom door slam, followed by a female muttering while stomping down the stairs. I would hear the front door get slammed by whoever it was on the way out. I didn't ask any questions, so he didn't have to lie or tell me the gory details of the events of the night before, most of which I had heard anyway.

I think that he wanted me out of his hair. Therefore, he let me please myself by traveling the world and spending his money on whatever I needed or wanted. I needed to keep myself out of his sight, pretty much. Which surprised me when I was all he had left now. Maybe he wanted to wallow in his self-pity every day. My mother died from a drug overdose when I was six. Two years ago, my brother Elias died after getting poisoned. His unknown killer has never been found nor brought to justice. His death gutted me and my father. Now that his son and heir to the family name was gone, it meant our reputation and line would die out, which added to his woes. I guess he didn't think me worthy of marrying one day and having children that could carry on the line. But it wasn't to be now. I was here and never going to escape.

That life was now gone, snatched away from me. Here I was, stuck in some dreary basement with an asshole in charge of my future. It smelled damp down here, and a foul odor emanated from somewhere. I couldn't pick out what it was. Was it the dank atmosphere of this wet concrete basement floor? Maybe it was the filth of the other women down here. Maybe in time, I would smell like that down here, too. I sighed; my arms chained to the wall were aching. No matter how much I tried, I could not find any relief.

Whatever my fate was going to be. I was sure it would not be one that I would like. I was optimistic about that. The other girls in the room were testimony to my fate. I wouldn't say I wanted to be judgemental, but it pained me looking at these poor naked women's dirty, unkempt appearances. I thought the same fate was in store for me, and it was not going to be pleasant. They had been prisoners here far longer than I had been. Their bodies were dark with dirt and dust, and goodness knows what else with their tear-streaked faces, bodies, and legs.

I've tried to find out more about where we were, who had taken them, and me. But no one will tell me anything. All I get is a grunt in response. I presume they're too traumatized, or they don't know either. They seemed too scared to tell me anything in response to any of my questions. I drew in a breath when I heard a key in the lock. I sucked in a breath with fear beginning to overtake me, and I shivered. I became more worried and fearful about what would happen next. Especially when I heard the other girls' bodies stiffen, and they began whimpering in fear. Whatever it was going to be, no doubt it wouldn't be a positive experience.

The iron door flew open, hitting the wall and letting off a metallic bang, making the room vibrate and jump, which caused us all, in turn, to shiver in fright and gasp with the loud noise. The thug on the other side strode into the room after flicking the switch, giving a meager glow from the one lightbulb in the room. He was well over six feet with a bald head and his body covered in tattoos since he felt confident enough to be shirtless around here. He was cocky and made himself look scary. You wouldn't want to meet this guy in some dark alley. He was that scary. He scanned the room until his eyes settled on me. My bottom lip began to quiver, knowing he was going to pick me, and I feared what my fate might be. Whatever it was, I was sure it would not be one to be enjoyed. Not again... I began panicking and pulling at the chains that bound me to the wall. However, I knew any struggle to escape was useless. I would no doubt be finding out my destiny shortly.

He walked over to where I sat on the damp floor chained to the wall. "Oh, it's good to see you're finally awake," he growled. He undid the locks, grabbing hold of my arms and yanking me up to my feet.

I was blindsided and gasped in pain. His actions made it feel like my arm was getting ripped out of its socket with his sheer strength.

He leered at me while dragging me across the room like a caveman did to his woman. Then he wrenched me out the door and pulled me up again until I stood straight. Then, we began our walk down the corridor.

But really, he walked while dragging me along since I couldn't keep pace with his long strides. "What do you want with me?" I demanded. I don't know where I found the strength to ask him anything. "Where the fuck are you taking me? "I demanded of this hellish brute. I got nothing in response while he continued dragging me down the long stone corridor toward my eventual doom. I kept stumbling while I struggled to keep up with him. I might be held here as a captive. But I would continue to be strong and fight the best I could.

Finally, down the end of the hall, he stopped when we came to a closed door. He unlocked and opened the door, throwing me into the room. I landed on my knees, scraping them on the damp stone floor. He slammed and locked the door behind me. Great! What fate awaited me now?

I leaned back on my knees and stared around the room, which was scantly furnished. It consisted of only two armchairs, a sofa along the wall, and an armoire. There was no escape. Even the windows had bars. Escape was impossible. There was nothing to do now but get me off this damp floor and grab comfort in one of the armchairs. I sat down, resigned to my fate, waiting for whatever fate brought me next. My stomach was churning with worry and hunger. I felt nauseous while I waited and began overthinking everything. Exhaustion finally overcame me. I felt my eyes slowly getting heavy with sleep, with the comfort of the armchair. It was a comfort I had not felt in a long time.

It was blissful compared to my current pose of lounging on the cold, damp stone basement floor chained to a wall. No wonder sleep finally overcame me, taking me to its deep, dark depths.

The next thing I knew... I was getting grabbed by my hair and roughly pulled out of the chair I was sitting in. "Owww, you're hurting me!" I yelled.

"I'm pleased to hear it. What do you think you're doing? I don't recall permitting you to sit in one of my chairs. It would be best for you to kneel on the floor before me where you belong quickly. NOW," I yelled when she wasn't moving quickly enough for my liking.

"It would be great if I had a heads up on the protocol. I would then know what was expected of me. But, instead, I was thrown in this room by some asshole who tossed me in here without any instructions," I huffed.

"Doing it today would be good if you know what's best for you, Girl, instead of being a brat and back-chatting me instead of obeying my instructions. It would be best if you were kneeling waiting for me to arrive. I want to see you kneeling there like a good girl waiting for me next time. Be ready for me to give you permission or instructions on what I would like you to do next. You are getting ideas above your station now, girl. You will do only what I tell you; otherwise, unpleasant things will come your way, my girl. I will promise you that."

"You are here to serve me and nothing else. You're lucky that you've turned out to be a first-rate specimen and easy on the eye," I told her while running my finger down her cheek. "You will go a long way with me if you behave." I smiled when she flinched at my remark. "Good girl. You're lucky. You now belong to me. I shall forgive you this indiscretion this one time since you are new. Any other master would not let you get away with this insubordination. I will not be letting anyone else touch you. I'm going to make you mine. Unlike those other girls, they aren't as fortunate as you. They get to have my men now that I have used them and am tired of them. Now, they belong to my men. When my men have had enough, I will eventually sell them at auction and ship them off to others that will take my dirty seconds." I laughed at her when I saw the expression of horror on her face.

I gulped, fearing what he meant by servicing him. In the back of my mind, I knew they would be of a sexual nature. I'm optimistic he might be gentle, but I didn't hold much faith in that observation.

"Now then, strip naked and kneel before me, girl. You better be quick about it, too. I don't want to be punishing you this early. I'm sure you don't want to sit on a sore, whipped ass on the basement floor. Who knows what infection you might catch."

It seemed being chained in a basement wasn't punishment enough for this guy. "What will happen if I don't?" I needed to poke the bear to see what he would let me get away with. I don't know where I pulled this courage from, or was it more like stupidity?

"Feisty little one, aren't you? You could be the best pet I have ever found. I'm warning you now; you will regret what happens if you don't behave." I tell her in a calm but threatening manner. I liked this girl. I might keep this girl until she got too old, or I got sick of her, whichever came first. "Try it and see what happens, girl. I'm certain you won't be able to sit down for a month if you want to test my patience."

I gulped down the lump in my throat. I better do what this Bossman asked of me. I stood up from the chair, took my clothes off, and placed them in a neat pile on the chair. I took a deep breath, ashamed to be naked in front of this stranger before me. Now, I watched and waited and wondered what fate would befall me. I walked over to where he stood when he crooked his finger in my direction to where he wanted me in front of him. I was staring down at the floor while I walked. I was too scared to look him in the eye. When his feet came into view. I knelt on the floor before him. I continued staring at the floor. I didn't want to stare up at him, afraid of what I might see if I looked at his face or into his eyes. Before I knew what was happening...

he grabbed my hair in one fist. "Owww," I yelled when he pulled my hair back, forcing me to gaze up at him.

I bent down, staring her in the eyes, blasting my hot breath over her, telling her between my clenched teeth. "Take my cock out. Please show me what delights you can do with those pretty lips and your hungry mouth. No biting either, or you will get the whipping of your life. I won't hold back if I'm not pleased with your performance."

Oh, God, anything but that. I was left with no choice. I had to do what he demanded of me. I raised my hands, which were shaking so badly. I struggled to undo his belt. It didn't help that it was holding his jeans up under his ample belly, hanging over it. With great difficulty, I finally managed to undo his belt, followed by his zipper.

I then struggled to pull his jeans down over his knees. I was hoping he might topple back and hit his head on something. If only. Then I could maybe make good my escape. Would I be that lucky? Nope, I'm sure he has armed guards everywhere in this place. Finally, able to get his jeans down past his knees, I reached for his boxers and pulled them down.

I pulled his boxers down to reveal his cock in its full glory. It bobbed menacingly around in my face with the sniff of freedom it got from the confinement in his pants. I gulped while I watched his giant cock with its twisted, bulging veins throbbing and pulsating at me right there in my face. I felt like it was there taunting and teasing me. I gulped, unsure what to do next.

I stood staring down at her, waiting for her to start sucking my hard, painful cock. When she grabbed me with her warm small hands, I nearly exploded on the spot expecting cum to shoot out all over her pretty face. What a sight to behold that would have been.

While I knelt there looking with disgust at his cock bobbing in my face. I grabbed it near the base squeamish, afraid of what to do next. I felt like he slapped me when he shouted at me...

"Girl, you better be quicker than this next time; otherwise, you will get a spanking or whipping for your insubordination," I growled at her. It was killing me the time she was taking with each step. I needed my cock deep in her hot mouth now already, sucking me hard before I filled her mouth with my cum. I hoped she took it all and swallowed it all without losing a drop.

"Y-y-y-yes," I stuttered. I grabbed his hairy, slightly flaccid canary bobbing around in front of my face. I was not at all enthusiastic about the task ahead. The bastard should use a lawn mower to manscape if he wanted this shit done to him. But I guess he didn't care. I was here to use and abuse. When he decided I was no longer useful to him, he would discard me like those poor girls in the basement.

I thanked God that I wasn't a virgin anymore. At least, that was one thing he couldn't take away from me. My boyfriend Nico was the one to whom I had given that pleasure. I missed him and knew I would never see him again. I could feel tears pricking my eyes, but I didn't want to give this bastard the satisfaction of my tears, thinking they were for him when they weren't.

I grimaced when grabbing that horrid hairy canary. I cringed when I began stroking him up and down with a half-hearted attempt and giving it a tentative lick when the precum started to leak from the tip of his cock. God knows how he was leaking precum when he wasn't even fully hard. I could feel the thick bulbous vein running down his cock spring to life and throbbing with his want and need. I squirmed when I could feel his cock growing harder and thicker between my fingers. I began massaging his horrific hairy sacs of semen with my other hand. I tried my best not to vomit with a distaste for the disgusting way they felt beneath my fingers.

"You need to get your act together and do better than that, girl. Otherwise, I will have to take matters into my own hands. I think I've given you enough warnings, my pet. So now I will," grabbing hold of her hair in my fist and tugging her head back. "Open that fucking smart mouth now, Bitch." I growled when she was reluctant.

I was pleased when she finally saw the error of her ways. I was thankful when she opened her mouth under duress, probably to scream. I took full advantage and rammed my giant cock deep into her mouth. That was the only thing that would keep her mouth quiet from the trash she kept spewing forth.

It delighted me to watch her sputter and choke on my cock while I held him down her throat. I felt elated when he began choking her, watching tears pour down her cheeks. Before I took some pity on her taking him out. I was going soft, letting her come up for air. "Breath while you can, girl, cos it's going to get stuffed full again in a minute," I laughed. It amused me no end watching her gasping for air, drool running down her chin, and tears running down her face. I watched it slowly dripping off her chin before landing on her luscious perky tits. God, that was so hot and sexy.

"Get ready, Girl, here I come again," I hollered before ramming him deep and hard down her fucking throat again, taking great delight in my actions. Oh, fuck me when she swallowed. I couldn't hold myself back any longer. "F-f-f-u-u-u-c-c-k-k," I roared. I grabbed her head to brace myself while coming deep down her throat. Fuck me dead; that felt amazing. I was never going to let go of this girl. She would be mine for all eternity now. I held him there, pumping everything I had deep down her throat. At the same time, it excited me while I watched her face turn red. I loved hearing her gag and watching the tears running down her face, turning me on even more. While she gagged, struggling to breathe, it turned me on while I spurted every drop of cum out of my cock.

When I had pumped every spurt of cum that I could down her throat. I pulled out. I smiled to myself, watching while she gasped for air. God, I was a sadist, but I loved it. I loved watching her making such a mess of her pretty face. I rubbed the top of her head, complimenting her for a job well done. "You're such a good girl for me, my pet."

It was a remarkable sight before me, with my cum and her spit going everywhere and drooling down her chin. Then, it began spilling over while she gagged some more, running in a stream down her body. The sight of her like this turned me on once again. I watched my cock become rigid in an instant. "Clean your mess up, girl. I wouldn't say I like it when my girl is a dirty mess. But first, you can clean my cock before your next feed of him."

"H-h-h-how do I do that?" I was at a loss. He didn't give me a towel or anything to clean up his mess. What was I supposed to do? I had never done this before; I didn't know what was expected.

"Use your imagination, girl. I'm sure you have a vivid imagination in that head of yours. Lick my cock clean with that filthy tongue of yours, and then use your fingers to wipe up the mess. Then suck them clean while I watch," I laughed, watching with great delight when her face became a mask of unimagined horror. I could see the disgust before my eyes, which brought immense joy to my soul. "Use your tongue? I leave my trusty cock in your hands."

Will someone please kill me now? I couldn't think of anything worse than digesting his disgusting cum mixed with my saliva. The little I had endured almost made me vomit. But I grabbed his cock, licking it clean of the cum and my spittle that covered it. Which nearly made me almost throw up again. I could feel the bile rising in my throat. His cum tasted disgusting salty and vile. I couldn't even begin to describe it... Ugh, then I had to clean it from my body and suck it from my fingers. It was bad enough that the amount he spilled down my throat made me feel like I needed to vomit. But, once again, I couldn't think of anything worse. Nothing like my lovely Nico's; at least his tasted edible. Whereas this dirty scumbag's cum tasted disgusting as he was.

I cringed when I began the unenviable task of scraping up the bits of his disgusting cum with my fingers off my body and the floor where it had fallen. I was wary about putting my fingers in my mouth and sucking them clean. While at the same time, I was trying not to vomit it back up when I did this. I hoped to do it all within a suitable time frame to avoid his wrath again. When I had finally finished the task given to me, he dished out his next set of orders.

" I've changed my mind. Get up on the sofa now," I demanded. "Get on all fours facing away from me," I told her. At the same time, I removed my boots, then pulled my jeans and boxers hanging around my ankles until now. I left my top half still dressed. There's no need to go all the way. I picked up my jeans, fishing a condom from my back pocket. I didn't want to take any chances. I hadn't had time to get the doctor to check her out or give her any contraception. When she was in the desired position, I slid my finger between her pussy lips and slid it up to her clit. "Goodness me, you are a wet little girl. You love this, don't you? It's making your pussy dripping wet for me. So willing to please me as your master, my little pet. You can always trust your body to betray you with its true feelings," I laughed. I suited up with my condom and rammed my cock deep and hard inside that tight hot wet pussy. I smiled when I heard her gasp when I hit home. "Oh fuck" that felt so amazing.

"Fuck, that hurt. Asshole... don't give me time to adjust to the size of your sizeable cock at all." I knelt there, taking it all. I was trying not to think about what he was doing to me. I wished he would hurry up and cum so this indignity could all be over. But, instead, he started pounding me faster and faster, going deep and hard. He was relentless, and it was taking a toll on me. Again, I wished he would just hurry up and cum in me so it could all be over. He finally stilled, and relief filled my body when he came deep into me. I thanked God, and now it was all over. I heard him grunt and then collapse on top of me, which caused me to collapse under him with his weight on top of me. "Hurry up and get off me, asshole? I can't breathe with your weight squashing me?"

I rose slightly and slapped her across the face. "You can wait, girl. Give me a moment to recover from my strenuous exercise, then I will. Don't be so rude. I'm in charge here bitch, not you. You need to learn your place in this establishment, okay? If you're not careful, I might choke you here until no breath is left in your body. It would be a damn shame if I had to kill you before I've had my fill of you and your delectable body. I'm the one in charge of you, not the other way round." Sheesh, was she a bossy bitch or what? She better watch herself around me, or she will pay dearly, maybe even with her life. She currently had me in a vulnerable position. Otherwise, I wouldn't be putting up with her behavior. I sighed, lifting myself off the top of her.

I pulled the condom off my now flaccid cock tying it up and throwing it next to her. "Get rid of that rubbish." I bent over, picking my clothes up off the floor. I began putting them back on, telling her. "Get up now. Pronto. Now hurry up and dispose of that rubbish like I instructed you to. Bin is over there," pointing to the corner where it sat. "Ice Pick will return you to your deluxe accommodation when you have completed that task after I have departed."

"Gee, thanks, asshole. First, you call me your girl. Then, tell me I'm only yours. Now you want to return me to that hell hole you took me from. No creature comforts or even a shower after doing all I did for you." I was unprepared for what he did next, which left me in total shock.

"I'm getting sick of your sassy mouth, girl." Anger coursing through my body from her backchat. I slapped her hard across the cheek with the back of my hand in my anger. Then, I smiled when I saw my red handprint glowing across her cheek. "Do I need to stick my cock in your mouth again? It seems to be the only time I can get you to be quiet." I had seen the red glow from my hand across her cheek. It now made me want to spank her ass and watch that turn from a lovely pink blush to a deep red glow across her ass.

I was pleased when she shook her head. No? I had stunned her into silence. "I'll only warn you once, girl. Keep this up; I will ensure you never get any creature comforts. You will be stuck in that basement forever. You will never be able to leave. I will use you until you're all used up. Then I won't want you anymore. I will let my men in to use you until you can take no more. Then my options will be to kill you or sell you to another body trader who will treat you worse than I will. Choose your course of action wisely here before you regret your decisions."

"Better still, maybe I'll throw you naked out on the streets to fend for yourself. I won't even give you the honor of selling you to your next master. You will need to earn your place and everything I expect or want of you in my house. You haven't done enough for me yet to give you any rewards. I'll take points off you for all the backchat you've given me today. Do I make myself clear?"

"Whatever," I mumbled to the asshole. It sounds like I need to behave better towards this asshole if I want to get anywhere in this place. It would be a step above that dirty, dark, damp basement where I'm currently being held prisoner. I picked up my clothes off the floor to put them back on. I was taking my time putting them on, trying to delay the inevitable. I wanted to delay my return to the basement as long as possible.

What was that? I didn't hear you?" I roared, making her jump. I almost scared myself since the room was so quiet.

"Yes, you have master," I whispered.

Damn, this girl is trying the extreme limits of my patience. Did I want all the bother of putting up with her and her actions? Hell, yes, I did. Although half of me was saying no. I had the other half and my cock telling me that I needed her. Because she was so damn good at taking my cock. Plus, her pussy was nice and tight, and she knew how to squeeze my cock just right. It felt amazing and made me cum much quicker than I would have liked. I'm sure she would be amazing at pleasuring me in other ways the more I thought about it.

I soon snapped out of my daydream when I realized what she was doing. "What the hell do you think you're doing?" I grabbed her by the arm. "What do you think you're doing? I don't recall permitting you to put your clothes back on. You're to be naked down there for your punishment for the backchat you've given me. I think you need to suffer some more before you get rewarded." I felt smug when she shook her head. She feared me with the look I observed on her face, which gave me even more pleasure at how I treated her. I could feel my cock twitching in my pants again.

I grabbed her by the arm, dragged her across the floor to the door, and opened it. Ice Pick should have stood guard outside the door, ready to deal with her after I had left. I growled and started dragging her down the hallway behind me. It looked like I would have to take her there myself. *Where had everyone disappeared to now?* Wait until I find out where those men had gone. I would demand to know why they weren't at their posts. Ice Pick knew better than to leave his post. He should be here waiting for me to finish with my pet. He better have a decent excuse for leaving his position. People would pay for their actions or inactions, whatever the case may be.

I dragged her behind me down the corridor, with her complaining all the way. Until we approached the door leading down to the basement. I opened the door and dragged her down the stairs behind me, bumping on every step we went down. With her complaints of me filling my ears about how I was hurting her while she bumped on each step. I was angry and annoyed now that she kept stumbling while trying to keep up with me. Now, she was pushing the boundaries of my anger. I thanked my lucky stars when we finally reached the bottom of the stairs.

I unlocked the steel door to where all the girls were chained. I cringed with the noise the door made when it creaked and echoed throughout the basement. I pulled her across the floor to her empty spot against the wall. I tossed her to the floor and grabbed hold of the chains. I grabbed one arm and put the cuff on. I picked up the other cuff and locked her arm on the wall. I was highly annoyed that I had to even step foot in this dark, dank basement due to my staff being absent. Then, the deed of having to lock her up. This was their job, not mine. I wouldn't say I liked entering the smelly hellhole down here. It was below my station stepping foot in here. This was their job, not mine, so I didn't have to come here. They better have a damn fucking good excuse for why they were not on duty. "Till next time, girl," I smiled, leaving her there. I hoped she suffered naked in the cold basement, which made me shiver with the cold even though I was fully clothed.

I glared at the other girls who dared to stare around at me. I grinned when they nearly gave themselves whiplash, looking straight back again. I surveyed the basement, wondering what other changes I could make in the cellar to worsen their discomfort. *Hmmm, a few bad ideas came to me. I'll have to put them into practice later.* I turned and exited the cell. I slammed the door shut, locked it, and went back upstairs... It was now time to find those men and where they had gone. I don't know what was happening. No one seemed to be around. It was too quiet for my liking. Whatever it was, my gut was now telling me it wasn't good. Maybe I should head for my secret safe room in case trouble had found its way here. Then I could observe from the CCTV cameras in there what was happening outside...

Chapter Four – Christa

I let out a loud sigh of desperation at my current doom. It seemed there would be no escaping from this place at all... Unless I could be a good girl and find my way to stay in his bedroom. That Bastard hadn't even let me get my clothes back on. They were now in a pile on the floor upstairs. I was shivering, and my teeth were beginning to chatter with the extreme cold and dampness down here. I got my hopes up when the door was flung open. Was it him? Did he miss me? Had he changed his mind and come back for me and take me out of here to spend more time with him? Horrid as he was, it was better to be with him in some comfort than sitting here doomed in this damp, dark basement.

When I turned to observe who was intruding on our torture chamber, I saw it was one of the guards with the girl who must have disappeared while I was upstairs with the grand master. He tossed her down the last few stairs. She landed in a crumpled heap on the bottom of the stairs in a puddle of water on the damp concrete. He unlocked the door, and the creak as it swung open hurt my ears. He picked her up and threw her through the doorway like a piece of trash. I guess that's all we were to these men. She landed with a thump on the floor, ending up in a heap in another puddle of water. He didn't even bother moving her to her cell to chain her up in her corner or shutting the door. Whatever he had done with her, he seemed to know she wouldn't be a problem before he returned. I could see she was an unconscious, bloody mess. At least, I hoped she was only unconscious and not dead. God knows what horrors she had just endured with that monster. I wished I could go and help her, but my chains made help impossible. This would be my eventual fate when he had tired of me, whoever this strange, dark, sadistic man was that held us all captive. He left as quickly as he arrived without regard for her or us.

I needed to try and keep myself sane throughout this ordeal. Sleep was impossible since the chains made lying on the basement floor impossible. I was cold since that asshole wouldn't let me bring my clothes or put them on. I tried to take myself away from the nightmare I currently found myself in. To take myself away from this nightmare that I was living. I lay my head against the cold brick wall and began reminiscing about the memories of my old life. I felt the need to punish myself even more, it seemed. No more would I ever experience the warm sun touching my face. The burn left as it lit my face along with the sting of the wind. Nor the breeze through my hair while I was driving my convertible through the streets of Europe. The current from the wind whipped my hair up, slapping me in the face. I felt pleasure in the sting it left when hitting my face. No more would I be feeling the sand beneath my feet. Nor the waves washing over my feet, causing my feet to sink into the sand. While my dress blew up in the breeze, revealing my panties beneath to whoever watched from afar.

I didn't have a care in the world back then. I was safe and living out the dreams of my life. Nights out dancing the night away with my girlfriends in the clubs. All that I had taken for granted. Little did I know that it would be all cruelly ripped away from me one day. Now, it was all a distant memory. I had been ripped out from my life of innocence straight into this one of horror and fear of the unknown. One I had never experienced nor ever dreamed I would ever find myself in my previous life. I had been drugged and then kidnapped on my way back from the toilet in the club. I had been grabbed after being drugged. I had been bundled out the back door and thrown into the back of a van. No one even came to my aid.

The next thing I knew when I came around. I found myself in the back of a dirty van, gagged with a rag, which caused me to gag and almost throw up. I tried to escape the two men, but they were too strong and overpowered me. I was then tied up and left helpless on the floor. They took great delight in speeding and turning corners at tremendous speed. I was getting thrown all over the van. I was full of bruises when we reached our destination, a private airport in the middle of nowhere. I was grabbed from their van after getting jabbed with a needle to knock me out again. The next thing I recall was waking up in this dark, dirty basement before I got taken upstairs to fulfill that man's hairy canary's needs.

I wondered what my dad was doing right now. Did he know I was missing? Would he even be searching for me? Would he even care? I'm sure he was sick at the thought of being unable to find me. I was all he had left... Would he ever be able to find me and discover who had taken me? Where I was now being held prisoner. I hoped that with all his resources, he might find me one day. I held onto that hope. I hoped it would help me through this nightmare I was currently living. Upon reflection, I thought about it. He never checked in on me daily or weekly. I was lucky some days that he even took my calls. At least when I rang to keep him in the loop of where I currently was and what I was up to.

I could hear banging coming from upstairs. I wondered what was going on up there. I was sure it sounded like multiple gunshots that I could hear in the distance. What the fuck is going on out there? I could feel my heart pounding in my chest with fear, wondering and waiting for what would happen next. Would whomever they were come and rescue us? Or worse, would they go after us and kill us all down here? Or had my father found me, and someone was going to rescue those other women and myself from these awful men? I could only hope.

Chapter Five: - Brazen

We rode out to Torres's compound. We made sure to dump our bikes and the two vans we brought to rescue the women hidden in the warehouse in the forest. We didn't want to alert them to our presence before we needed to. We separated into two groups, hiking through the forest unchallenged. It was too easy, which was a worry. It seemed that Torres would never expect anyone to come and attack his compound from the woods. We walked around the compound wall to the front since we knew there to be no entry from the back. He only had two sentries on guard out the front of their compound. No challenge to us. Too busy laughing at something amusing to them on their cell phones. Idiots! Two of my closest men crept along with stealth, grabbed them from behind by the throat, and slit their throats. They were both down before they knew what hit them.

We remained hidden as best we could while we peered through the gate. We needed to know roughly how many men were on duty outside the main house to ensure we weren't outnumbered. How many men did we have to deal with? There appeared to be about six men outside patrolling the courtyard. We searched the men we had downed at the gate to see if one of them had a key for the gate. We hit pay dirt, finding a set in the back pocket of one of the dead men.

We tried the keys, and luck was on our side! Success was ours when the first key we tried fit the lock perfectly. I opened the gate. I opened it as quietly as possible since I didn't want to alert them to our presence. I opened the gate as far as possible, hoping they wouldn't squeak. I only opened it wide enough for us to fit through. Then, we took them all by surprise when all my men stormed through the open gate. This resulted in the men inside scattering like roaches in the light. We all followed them, taking them out one by one with a snap to the neck or a knife to the throat. It depended on which of my men's particular skill sets was at play. We managed to get them all down before anyone could raise the alarm to anyone inside. This didn't mean there weren't any security cameras in play. Therefore, we still had to guard against any surprise attacks. I knew Torres wasn't stupid. Well, most of the time, anyway.

Once we had taken down all the outside men, we regrouped, planning our next move. We were fully aware of our surroundings, constantly looking for surprises from other guards. We needed to wait and discover if other guards might come out after us. They would indeed have the whole compound under surveillance. I told all my men, "Mo' and I will go to the basement. We needed to assess how many women are down there and their current situation. Meanwhile, you guys check out the rest of their compound; if you find Torres, he's mine. You can capture him, but leave him for me to finish off. Also, Doc oversees everyone upstairs, so listen to him," I emphasized to the men.

Mo and I both crept down the stairs to the basement. We were surprised to find they had no men guarding the basement door. Still, they weren't expecting anyone, especially not us. It wasn't like the women could escape the locked room either. Mo managed to pick the lock on the door. Yes, I fist pumped when the door was open, and we could now enter. It was dark inside, meaning we couldn't see a thing. I fished my cell out of my pocket and turned the torch on, holding it up to survey the room.

Omg, those poor women. What the hell had they suffered and endured here? They were all chained to the wall, filthy, along with matted hair. Except for one, although she was dirty, it was apparent she hadn't been here as long as the other women. On the other hand, it was clear the others had been here for a while. God knows what Torres and his men had done to them. Although I could hazard a guess, none of it was good. "Given that there are only five women here. We'll take them to Sherry at the refuge, Mo. I don't want to traumatize them further by returning with them to my compound."

I was pleased when Mo nodded in agreement. I went to move and almost tripped over a woman lying in a heap on the ground in the dark. Luckily, I saw her at the last moment before I did any more damage to her, tripping over her. "Geez, make that count, six women." I bent down to feel for a pulse to make sure she was still alive and not dead. It was faint, but I did feel a slight thready pulse there. She was barely hanging on, but she was still here for now. To add insult to injury, they had left her in a dirty puddle of water. I pulled her out of the puddle and removed my jacket to give her some warmth. I stood up when I felt the hairs suddenly sticking up on the back of my neck.

I checked around to ensure no one followed us to the basement. It appeared that no one had. But where was this feeling coming from? I was taken aback. It felt like a soul was calling out to me here in this room. How was this possible? It felt like my soul mate, whom I never knew I wanted, was here. She was here in this room. With me now. What the hell was happening to me? I had never felt like this before. This was partly due to severe childhood trauma after witnessing what my father did to my mother—her constant beatings before he killed her one night in front of me. I was never the same again. My heart closed off with a steel vice to anyone and everything. I could never get hurt if I didn't get close to anyone. I had never felt love again after my mom died, and I never wanted to. I had survived this far without it and didn't know what it was. Therefore, what you didn't know, one didn't miss.

This wasn't me. I had never needed anyone. Until now... I scanned the room, and I found her there she was... Poor thing, she was sitting in the cage nearest to me, naked and shivering. She was doing her best on this damp basement floor chained to the wall. Despite her dirty hair, she seemed different from the other women in the room. She was the one that hadn't been here the longest. I could tell. She didn't appear to be as traumatized as the other women. She was new, and they had seen and suffered more than she had. She was staring over her shoulder, staring in my direction. Her eyes pleaded with me to save her and not harm her. Our gazes lingered over each other. It was like a magnet; I couldn't pull myself away from her eyes.

Despite all this, she was the most stunning siren I had ever seen, and her soul was calling out to me. *I will save you, baby. I will never hurt you.* I hoped that I was showing back to her with my eyes I was there for her. I am not here to harm you, baby. I'm here to save you and make you mine. I am here to protect you and never allow anyone to hurt you again. But then, will you be safe from me? I didn't know why. What did the universe have in store for me? For us now? I noticed she had the most striking, vivid amber eyes. Her golden orbs shimmered in the dim light, bright like a melted pot of the finest gold. They commanded my attention, and everything around me now faded away. All I could see and feel in the room was her. When I thought I had hit rock bottom, she was like a fire, ready to melt the ice within my heart. It felt like my soul had found its mate, and I was here solely to rescue her.

Nothing nor anyone else existed in this room anymore. I could feel those eyes begging and calling for me to save her. She had called me, and I had come for her. I would answer. I needed to be close to her. I needed to see her soul through her eyes. I had to have her. She couldn't go back to Sherry's shelter. My stunning siren was calling to my soul to take her with me. She was making me weak where no one else had before.

I felt my cock beginning to stir in my jeans. Even he was feeling this emotion, too. But now was not the time. Geez, down, boy. Please don't embarrass me now. This is not the time nor the place for this dance. Another time and another place...

****

Suddenly, I felt the hairs on the back of my neck stand up. I felt my body shiver at the change in the atmosphere in the room. One that this man commanded in the small space. I could feel him coming across the room towards me, but he was still near the cell door. He was still standing like a statue while staring at me. How was this possible? I had felt him before I saw him. I could feel prickles of electricity running along my skin the closer he got. Now that he was moving at great stride in my direction. Why did he have this effect on me? My soul mate had come to rescue me. Was this even possible, and it was happening? I gasped when he got close. The feeling in the air had turned electric. I took in a deep breath when he knelt next to me.

The electricity buzzed between us in the atmosphere. That voice… When he spoke, the hairs on my scalp rose with the electric atmosphere in this room. The timbre of his voice vibrated through me, making me feel vulnerable and exposed. Yet he had me hooked. What trickery was this afoot?

The next thing I knew, I was rushing across the remaining distance between us. I strode across the floor to her in only four steps. I felt the need to be close to her. I knelt at her level, watching her cower and cringe when I got close. "I'm sorry. I never meant to scare you." I worried about what I was doing being so close to her. I felt like I was rushing her now, and she had been traumatized in this place. I was moving too fast. I knew now. But God only knows what Torres had put her and these other women through while being held hostage here.

"Hey," I whispered. "Please look at me, gorgeous," I begged of her. "I'm not here to hurt you. We've come to rescue you all and remove you from this hell hole. You're coming back with us. I'll keep you safe. No one will ever hurt you again. I promise, beautiful."

I saw her peek coyly at me through her eyelashes to see if I was telling her the truth. But she must've felt the trust in what I was telling her. She surprised me when she nodded in agreement with my statement.

"Is this your usual pickup line?" I smiled at this stranger. Even though I had been through hell in this place, I felt I could trust this man. I felt things that I had never felt for anyone before. Not even with my boyfriend, surprisingly.

I admired this woman despite all she had no doubt been through and where she was. She had a slice of humor still shining through despite everything she may have been through. I ran my knuckles down her cheek and grinned. My, my, she was a feisty one even under these circumstances. "No. I don't have one. Do you trust me?" I asked in a gentle voice. I loved her sass despite the dire situation she was in here. Then, add to her horrific situation these two strange men in the equation roaming the basement. I admired her strength. She managed to find some humor in this situation she had found herself in.

Once again, she nodded at me, seemingly scared to speak now, which was perfectly understandable under the current circumstances.

Who was this man? Why did he make the hair stand up on the back of my neck in excitement? I felt a shiver pulse through me. Even this close, he did things to my body I didn't or couldn't understand. I was wary of taking myself out of one hell hole into another. Despite everything... I felt I could trust this man. I was glad he had come to save me. I would never have to serve that other horrible, disgusting man again. I would never have to step into this dark, dank basement again. Who knows what his plan might be? He might want to put us in his basement for all I know, despite his words of reassurance that he was here to rescue us. Somehow, I didn't think that was his plan. I felt sure he was here to give me and the other women imprisoned with me a new life away from this place.

"My friend Molotov, or Mo for short." I grinned at the puzzlement across her face when she heard his name. "Yeah, don't ask. That's his story to tell you. First, don't take too much offense if he never does. You're coming home with me, okay? I never want to let you out of my sight again. I hope you will agree with me on that proposition. I promise I will also bring the other girls with us since it's late. They'll be coming to my house for the night too, okay? We need to get you all away from this place and soon. Before these men come back since they want to sell you. We need to hurry before they return.

In the morning, we'll take the other ladies to my friend Sherry's place, who runs a women's shelter. They'll be safe there with her, okay? She'll take care of them and provide housing when they're ready to leave her establishment." I needed to reassure her they would all be safe while running my index finger down her cheek.

I nodded, "w-w-why am I staying with you and not them?" I asked him in a shaky voice. I felt scared now that he was going to separate me from the other women. Despite everything that happened here, it felt like they were my rock in this place. I knew I could trust him but feared going somewhere new with this strange man.

"When I entered this basement, I felt my soul calling out to yours even in the dark. I hope you felt it in you, too. I feel I need you with me. I'll keep you safe, and no one will ever harm you again. I make that promise to you. I thought I had reached rock bottom in my life. I was cold and in a dark place. But now you're here like a fire to my soul, ready to melt the ice. I need you and will protect you forever, my gorgeous girl. No one will ever touch or have you again. I'll protect you. However, if you wish, you can go with them to the women's shelter if it makes you feel better. But I feel a need to have you in my life. I hope you also need to have me in your life. I feel I will better protect you under my roof."

"Okay," she nodded in agreement. "I don't know why, but I feel that I can trust you and your men. I don't think you're here to hurt us, or you would have done so already."

I sighed with relief when she told me she trusted me and my men...

"I do want to come with you, Mister. You are a charmingly handsome man with the need to protect me. I realize that now," waving my hand around him. "I feel I can trust you. Will you be okay with what they've done to me here? Now that I am virtually soiled goods thanks to that horrible man. Plus, I will need time to overcome my traumatic experience here."

"You can have all the time in the world you need, my sweetness. I hate what they have done to you and the other ladies here. I will never do that to you, my gorgeous girl. I'm not trying to downplay what happened to you. I want and need you to be in my life forever. I'd feel lost without you now that I've found you. I want you to be mine. My name's Brazen. Do you have a name, gorgeous?"

"It's nice to meet you, Brazen. Yes, my name is Christa." I pressed my fingers to my forehead while I decided what I wanted to do now. *Do I go with him or stay with the other women?* "Okay, Brazen, I will trust you and come with you and stay with you at your place. But if I need to go and stay with the other ladies, I hope you will trust me to go. Trust that I will return to you when I get over whatever I feel. You have me curious about you. Also, you're making me feel things I have never felt for anyone before. But I am warning you now. The moment you throw my past back in my face for whatever reason. I'll be out the door and be gone from your life forever. I will never have anything to do with you anymore."

"Never. I will never do that to you, gorgeous, even if we have the biggest fight of our lives. However, I know here in my heart," pounding my fist on my chest over my heart. "We will never fight."

"Okay, now get me out of these chains I'm trapped in. They're keeping me from you. It will leave me free to come with you," holding my chained hands. I was ready for this man to do whatever he needed—anything he needed to get me out of these chains. "Then take me out of this horrible place forever." I shivered both with the cold and the anticipation of what was to come in my future.

"Hey, Mo," I called out when I stood up. "What have we got to get these women unchained? Also, we need to find something to keep them warm." I wondered what he was thinking when I saw he had been watching our interaction. When I noticed he had his finger pressed against his chin in puzzlement.

"I'm on it already," I muttered, trying to see if I could pick the lock on the chains that imprisoned them.

"Don't worry, ladies," I tried to reassure them. "I promise we are here to rescue you all. We hope to get you out here as soon as we can. I plan to take you to my friend Sherry, who runs a women's shelter. She will help fix and heal you while providing food and shelter. She will give you all the tools to start a new life away from here. Please trust us to get you out of here and come with us. We might need to house you at my place tonight since it will be late when we finish up here and get home. If you decide to run now, you might find yourself in the clutches of Torres and his men. I'm not trying to scare you. I'm trying to be honest with you and give you the truth. You're scared, and I get that. You have every right to be. We're strangers to you, asking much of you to trust us where Torres and his men have mistreated you. The rest of my men are upstairs trying to find and sort out Torres and his men. We'll wait here until they've cleared upstairs. We must ensure it's safe to leave the basement before we head back upstairs again."

I crossed my legs and sat on the floor near my gorgeous girl. At the same time, I watched and waited for Mo to free Christa first, followed by all the women who needed to be from their chains. I was beginning to wonder what was going on upstairs. It all seemed too quiet upstairs. No one had bothered to come downstairs to check on the women to see if the women were still there. I'm sure we will get word shortly about what is going on. I was trying not to think of the alternative that my men had got rounded up. But then I imagine someone from here would have come to check on the women. Or worse still, Torres and the rest of his men had managed to escape. Either that, or they had already left to do their dirty deeds at another location before we arrived.

Like the champion, he is Mo persevered, picking at the locks with deep concentration and unlocking their chains individually. I watched the women rub their wrists in the same spot once free—no doubt in pain and from chafing from their chains. I was glad they trusted us enough to stay and not run away. The real test would come when it was time to leave. I breathed a sigh of relief when he finally had everyone unlocked.

Once they were free, including my precious angel, I told him to go upstairs while I stayed here with the women. "Let me know if you need me up there if we're outnumbered. Oh, and don't forget to find something for the woman to keep warm if possible."

"Will do, Prez. Sounds quiet up there. Too quiet, I'm getting rather concerned. It's either good or a massacre up there," I agreed.

"I know that's what I'm worried about." I watched while he stepped stealthily up the stairs, taking note of his surroundings and his gun pointed ready should he encounter any enemy. When he opened it, he was alert and prepared to face whatever was on the other side of the basement door.

Chapter Six: - Brazen

Although it seemed like he had been gone for hours, Mo eventually returned with an armful of blankets. "All clear, Boss. We appear to have won the battle above. We have all Torres's men that were left all secured. We'll load them in another van; alternatively, we could leave them locked down here. That way, we won't have to dispose of them. Torres and his top men don't seem to be here. They got away when they saw us coming. Failing that, Torres has a panic room on the compound. Alternatively, they weren't here and were away doing other dirty deeds and already gone before we arrived. In that case, we better leave here as soon and quickly as possible before they return."

"Okay, round all our men up and send two to bring our vans here. We'll need them to transport the women. You can go with them and send Doc down here. He can stay with me and give them a quick check-over, especially our unconscious woman. He can also monitor them for any medical intervention required when we safely have them in the van. Our other men can lock the men we've rounded up in the basement and leave them to Torres to sort out. Less work for us to do. We can hopefully be well on our way home when he returns. We won't have to worry about loading those assholes and disposing them at the other end."

"If you're sure that you can trust Doc Braze? I don't mind staying here with you."

"Yeah, I trust him out of everyone after you. It's not that I don't trust you, Mo. You're my right arm. I'd rather have you round up the men and take charge of the upstairs section. I trust you to do that for me if there are any surprises. But of course, you're the only one I ever trust for that duty apart from myself," I smirked. "You're the best eyes and ears I have, Buddy. I'd trust you with my life; you know that."

He nodded in my direction, lifting his chin, and disappeared back up the stairs. I could see the disappointment in his eyes at my request. I'd make it up to him later. It was that I didn't trust Mo; I knew I could trust him to keep my other men in line. I didn't know how they'd react and needed guidance for our plan to move out of this place without any more problems. I didn't know what their reaction would be if there were any more surprise attacks. We didn't know where Torres's men had disappeared, and I didn't know when they would return. We needed to leave now. It would take either Mo or me with them to direct them. Torres, still being out there, whereabouts unknown, was my biggest worry. "Hey, Mo"

"Yeah," he responded in a hopeful tone.

I wouldn't say I hated the trust and hopeful look in his eyes that I was about to ask him to stay with me. "No, not that." I frowned. "I will make it up to you later, I promise. But, before you leave, see if you can also round up some jackets for the women to keep them warm. I want to help them maintain some of their dignity after everything they have been through. I wouldn't want the other men seeing them like they are," raising my eyebrows at him. I hope he understood my need to care for the women currently trusting us with their care.

"Yeah," he looked away and left through the basement door. He was leaving me alone with the women until he came back. "Thanks for trusting me, ladies. I'll get you all out of here as soon as possible, okay?"

They were too scared to look me in the eye but were able to nod their affirmation of my plan.

Mo hadn't been gone long when he returned with some hoodies to add to the blankets that he already had that he'd found upstairs. "I found these hoodies too. I took them to give the women some more dignity and keep them warm apart, as well as the blankets."

"You're an exceptional man, Mo. You'll make someone a wonderful husband one day." I grinned when he grunted in response. It amused me to poke the bear. I watched the woman smile at him when he handed them their hoodie to go with their blanket to keep warm.

"What's happening upstairs, Mo?" I was now curious about what was happening upstairs.

"We've got all the men that were here. The other important ones we wanted the most appear to have either left before we arrived or not long after. For all we know, they could even be hiding in a panic room here. His men are staying loyal and not talking. Once we've got the ladies out into the vans, we'll bring the assholes down here to rot in hell."

"Okay. Send a couple of the men to get our vans and drive them round here. We need to leave as soon as they get here with the vehicle. Meanwhile, keep searching while I stay down here protecting the women. I want to know when the van rocks up, and then we're out of here. All the others can go collect our bikes hidden in the woods and return them to the compound later. Let me know when they arrive."

"On it, Prez. I'll organize the cleaners to eliminate the other piles of shit lying around the place. I'm hopeful they won't get disturbed before the others return here. Be back soon."

"Yeah. Let us be positive here. He'll wait a while before returning if he knows we're here. He's a piece of chicken shit."

"Isn't that the truth, Braze."

"Do you think we were too hasty killing them? Should we keep one to torture to get some intel from them about the operation here? Rather than leave them here in the basement?"

"Nah. I can sniff out another weak one upstairs to keep and torture later. I'll be able to smell the fear radiating off that one person. Then I'll tie them up and throw them in the back of one of the vans."

I laughed, shaking my head at him. "I'm sure you will, Buddy. I'm sure you will. You never stop amazing me with your skills."

Chapter Seven - Brazen

It wasn't long before I heard the men return with our van. "Okay, ladies, are you ready to move? Anyone not able to walk a great distance and need help?" I watched as the two women in the worst condition raised their hands. "Okay, ladies, I'll wait for Mo to come back down, then we'll help carry you up the stairs and out to the vans. I was beginning to give up hope of Mo coming back down and was ready to go back upstairs in search of him. Luckily, as I was about to take the stairs, he came rushing through the door. "Sorry for the delay, folks. I wanted to sweep the place before leaving to ensure it was safe."

"Mo. Two of our ladies need help walking out to the van. Grab a couple of our most trustworthy men and get them to help them out to the van. You can oversee our unconscious charge here. I know you'll be gentle with her. We'll get the doc to check her out now to ensure she can travel. Then, do a proper assessment when we get back to the compound.

After that, the others who are able can go out under their own steam. I don't suppose you mind grabbing some more helpers, Mo, to give you a hand taking these other two ladies up. I'll manage the other ladies and take them to the van."

"I'm on it, Boss. I'll be back soon," he raced back up the stairs as time was of the essence before he returned with Doc to help.

"You two go first, then we'll follow behind. Doc came over and checked over our unconscious charge. Though he wasn't happy with her condition, she was in a bad way. But it was best to do a pickup and run with her. After that, he would do a proper check and assess if he could help her or work things out to cover us if she needed further medical help. Once Mo and Doc had grabbed the two ladies and started back upstairs, I sprang into action. "I think we'll wait for

Mo to return and take your friend out to the van," I warned them. "Then we'll follow close behind them."

Mo was back in no time and wrapped the woman in a blanket, carrying her with great care up the stairs. "Ladies first..." I waved my hand for them to go up the stairs first while I followed up at the rear to keep them safe. I kept alert with my gun ready should I need to use it. While I constantly checked our surroundings to ensure no one was hiding to surprise us. We were prepared to do anything, but if we let our guard down...

We made it to the van without incident. Everyone helped to load the ladies in and belted them up in their seats. Mo had placed the unconscious woman on the back seat, laid her down, and belted her in. He got in the front to drive the van while I kept alert to our surroundings while maintaining a visual on the ladies. I wanted to make sure they were okay and traveling well...

I couldn't help peeking at my little vixen repeatedly and smiling when she caught me. I made her smile when she rolled her eyes at me when I'd pull a pouty face at her. I was pleased with myself that I made her smile. I couldn't wait until I got home to keep her safe at my compound. I'd get Doc to check all the ladies out to ensure they weren't hiding unseen injuries. Any who did would get checked out by Doc first and given the necessary care. Before I make the final call to take them to Sherry's shelter in the morning. I needed to ensure they were all in good health and not traumatized by their time in Torres's basement. It was my duty of care to care for them. I'll make another hefty donation to Sherry. I want to ensure she has enough funds to watch for my new ladies. Plus, any other ladies she has now and in the future.

I thought we were getting followed at one stage; thank goodness it was a false alarm. We arrived at my compound shortly after dusk and entered the gate without incident. I felt relieved once inside that we had got the ladies here in one piece. "Listen, ladies, here's the plan.

We'll get you inside and get you fed. Then you can shower, and I'll find some clothes for you." I got out and waited.

Mo got out, picking his charge off the back seat and carrying his unconscious charge into the house. He entered the hallway, went up the stairs to the second floor, and took her to one of the guest bedrooms. He then returned to help Doc help with the two ladies who needed help moving. I wanted to pick up my sweetheart and carry her in. I thought better of it since I didn't want to single her out for special treatment and make the other two ladies feel left out. I helped them out of the van, taking them by the hand. I helped them up the front stairs and into my home.

We entered the kitchen. This was where I found Valeria, my cook and housemaid. She was busy heating some chicken noodle soup for us all to eat. I could also smell the delightful smell of bread cooking in the oven. She was a miracle worker. I don't know what I'd do without her. "Please, ladies, sit at the table; we will get some food in you shortly." While I went to the cupboard, I got bowls and plates out to help Valeria and placed them on the countertop, ready for her to dish the food out. I grabbed some cutlery from the drawer and put it on the table. Then I sat down next to Christa since I started feeling famished myself smelling the soup.

Chapter Eight - Brazen

Despite the silence in the room, I was pleased that the ladies didn't hold back and managed to get some food down in their bellies. Once we had all eaten, it felt good to know that all the ladies were safe and we had brought them out of that place, away from Torres and his wicked ways. Along with the terrible conditions Torres had placed them in. Goodness knows what other atrocities they suffered at the hands of Torres and his men that we didn't know about. When everyone had finished eating, I asked Valeria to take the ladies upstairs, show them their rooms, and show them where the bathrooms were so they could freshen up and change into clean clothes.

I went upstairs to my bedroom and lay down on my bed. I texted Sherry to send some clothes over for the ladies. I would arrange for one of the men to collect them from her shortly. It meant they would have them to wear in the morning. I could care for them overnight and bring them to her shelter in the morning after they rested.

Sherry, ever efficient, texted back straight away.

On it. See you soon. Always happy to help you out. Thank you very much for another generous donation, Brazen.

B: **Thank you for doing this for the ladies for me. We're always happy to help you and your good cause. Thank you for all you do for these women. Don't hesitate to let me know if you're ever short on funds.**

S: **Thank you. I hate to take advantage of you.**

B: **Never, I promise, my fave compassionate lady.**

S: **You're making me blush now.** ☺

B: **Good. Just kidding! Sorry, not sorry.** ☺

S: **You always make me smile. Night**

B: **Night**

Valeria knocked on my door and informed me that the women were all in bed for the night.

"Thank you, Valeria," I called back. I texted Mo: **Drive to Sherry's and pick up some clothes for me for the women. She has put some aside for us to give the women in the morning.**

Mo: **Leaving now. I'll see you in the morning.**

I turned the light out and tried to get to sleep, ready to make an early start in the morning. Sleep evaded me while I tossed and turned all night. It was hard knowing that my gorgeous girl was nearby. No matter how much I wanted to be there with her, I knew it wasn't a good idea. I needed to give her time to get over her trauma. I don't know what trauma she suffered at the hands of Torres. Therefore, I would let her sleep alone like the other woman. I would give her some peace and hopefully get her through the trauma she and they had suffered. I knew placing them with Sherry would be the best scenario for them. She would provide them with all the help and services required to help them start over again.

Unable to sleep due to my mind working overtime as usual and unable to be quietened. I knew my beautiful, sweet girl was nearby. Even though she was safely ensconced in another part of the house with the other women, I could still feel her presence in my room. I needed to give her time to heal and recover from her trauma. Much as I wanted to hold her in my arms, I knew now was not the time. I needed to give her time and space to heal.

Exhaustion must have finally overcome me near dawn since I don't remember anything after that. Not until I heard noises of people stirring and moving around in other parts of the house. I stretched and yawned. I better get up, shower, and make myself presentable to the people in this place. After breakfast, I would call Sherry to arrange a convenient time to bring all the women to her refuge. I put another $20k donation in her account to help with the women and any others she would get through to help them recover and set up for the future.

I'm sure she could use every penny she could get. I got up, dragging my sorry tired ass into the bathroom.

I turned the shower on full blast until it was as hot as I could bear on my skin. I got in, standing underneath, feeling the needles of water raining down on me. I savored the sensation of the pins and needles while they rained down across my back. It made me wonder if Torres would be pissed at me since I had virtually taken these women from him right under his nose. Hopefully, he might never find out who it was. Although I was in no doubt that he probably had CCTV cameras all around his compound so he would know it was me. But I was glad the men and I had saved those women's lives from misery and hell under his rule.

When the water started running cold, I got out. I grabbed a towel off the rail, dried myself off, and dressed, ready for the day ahead, before I headed downstairs to grab a coffee and a smoke before eating breakfast.

Chapter Nine – Brazen & Christa

Once my shower was over, I dried off and grabbed my clothes to put on. I needed to make myself presentable for our lady guests. I hoped the men were behaving themselves downstairs around them, too. Better still if they were staying away for now. I went downstairs to the kitchen to grab a coffee before I went for my usual heart-starter cigarette on the back veranda. "Morning, ladies. I trust you all managed to sleep well." I nodded at them on my way past to the outdoors.

"Yes. Thank you," they all chorused.

"I'm glad I managed to get you all out of that terrible basement Torres had you encaged in. I'm glad you will get a new chance at life with Sherry. She will be great at helping you along your new journey. Now, if you will, please excuse me. I will take my coffee out on the veranda." I gazed across the table for my gorgeous girl, catching her blush when she noticed me seeking her out. I smiled and glanced away before anyone saw us staring at each other.

I hope she will trust me enough as god help me. I want to wake up next to her in my bed for the rest of my life. I cleared my throat, walked to the patio sliding door, and exited the rear veranda. I placed my coffee on the table while I grabbed my packet of smokes from the pot in the middle and pulled one out.

After putting it in my mouth, I grabbed my lighter and lit my cigarette. I sucked in a deep breath, and inhaling, I felt the rush of the first heart starter for the day. After exhaling, I picked my coffee up, taking a large gulp. I placed my right leg on the bench and rested my elbow on my knee, glancing across the back garden. I stood up with haste when I heard the sliding door behind me side open. I turned around to see who it was and blinked when I saw it was her. I smiled her way. "Morning, gorgeous. What brings you out here?"

My eyes flickered over him, wondering how I would answer his question. I had never felt a pull toward a person like this in my life before. I didn't know what was happening nor why I wanted him. "I just wanted to say thank you for rescuing us. I wanted to let you know that I trust you with my life. I appreciate all that you're doing for the ladies and me."

"You're welcome, Gorgeous. The pleasure is all mine. I hated seeing you like that in his basement. I will do all I can and hope I never see you or the other lovely ladies again in that situation. I hope that I never let you down. I would give up everything I owned to be with you if that's what it costs me."

"Wow," I wasn't sure how to respond to his words, and my eyes darted all around, looking everywhere but at him. "You've given me a reason to smile again. I know it's early days. I don't know why. But you matter to me. I can't explain it. We were soul mates in a previous life, maybe. Now we've finally found each other again."

"I'm glad I'm not the only one feeling this too. You've given me a reason to smile and feel something for someone. Something I thought I would never feel for anyone again. All I want is for you to be mine, gorgeous. I will treat you like a princess. No scratch that you deserve to be my Queen. I apologize for never formally introducing myself to you, my gorgeous girl. My name is Brazen."

"Pleasure to meet you, Brazen. My name is Christa," I beamed across at him.

"Do you have any family, gorgeous? Do you need me to contact anyone for you?"

"No, I don't think so. I have my dad. But I don't think he cared much for me after my mom and brother died." I stared wistfully into the distance, mourning that I no longer had them in my life. I never felt so alone in my life until now.

"I'm so sorry, Honey. What happened to them? Car accident?" I enquired.

"No, my mom died from a drug overdose when I was younger. I don't know if it was by accident or on purpose. I always wonder if she was murdered and if my father was behind it. He never married again, whether through guilt or losing the love of his life. Many have tried to catch his eye, but he's turned them all down. All he ever seems to want these days is a one-night stand. He's never with the same woman twice. Then, a couple of years ago, my brother was murdered. Someone poisoned him. They tried to blame suicide for his death. But I know he would never take his own life. He got mixed up with some bad people and paid the price for something he must have done wrong in their eyes. But they're no longer investigating his death since they considered it suicide. Maybe Dad does love me in his way.

But he sent me to boarding school. Then, when I graduated, he sent me off touring Europe with my friends. I got drugged and kidnapped on a night out with my friends. The next thing I knew, I found myself in that asshole's basement. Until you guys came along and rescued us. Now, here we are. Now that you know my story, what does your life story sound like?"

"Now, I don't want to disappoint you. Sorry that I can only give you the basics with me. My dad raised me since my mom died when I was young. My mom got killed in front of me when I was about ten years old. So, since my father never really cared and left me to my own devices. Until I manage to find myself, it's just me and my men."

"That's it? How did you guys get together?" I was curious to know, but would he tell me?

"Maybe one day I will tell you. But today is not that day."

"Okaaaay," I said, trying not to sound too disappointed.

I reached across, grabbed her hand, and pulled her closer to me. "I'm not trying to fob you off or be mysterious, gorgeous. It's hard for me to talk about things. It wasn't all easy and plain sailing to get here. But we will get there. I will tell you one day. Please understand."

I sighed, breathing in her scent, which did me in. I wanted to kiss her but didn't want to push her yet. I needed to give her time.

"Sure, take all the time you need, Brazen." I pulled away from him and returned to be with the other girls. I was disappointed he wouldn't share more with me, but it was what it was the end of the story, it seemed. But I guess he did have his reasons no need for me to be shitty about it, but it was too late now. I had left him looking lost and sad on the veranda with his coffee and cigarette.

Fuck I screwed that up. Now she hates me. Do I follow her in or stay out here and give her some space? Damn it, I'll finish my cigarette and then go in and make amends. I drank my coffee and finished my smoke before stubbing it in the ashtray. I exhaled that last drag and took a deep breath before letting it out through my mouth. Well, here it goes. It's now or never. I walked over to the sliding door and slid it open. Disappointed when I saw she was nowhere to be seen. The other ladies were still sitting at the table chatting amongst themselves, but my gorgeous girl wasn't with them. Damnit! I smiled at the ladies and dipped my chin. I walked away to look upstairs to see if she had returned to her bedroom, pissed at me for not answering her question to her satisfaction.

I knocked at her door. No answer. I turned the handle. Good, she hadn't locked it. I entered the room to see if she was maybe taking a shower. Nope, there was no sign of her since the bathroom door was open. No sign of her in there, and she wasn't in the bed. Hmmm, where could she have gone? I walked downstairs to the library in case she found her way there. She looked like she might be a reader. I wasn't wrong. She sat in one of the chairs with her nose deep in a book. I cleared my throat and told her, "I'm sorry."

She looked around over her shoulder at me. "Why? No need to apologize. Therefore, please don't be sorry on my behalf."

"I thought I might have upset you when I didn't answer your question satisfactorily."

"No, not at all. I'm just tired. I didn't sleep well. The bed was too soft after sleeping on a damp basement floor. Not that I slept well there either," I quipped in a bitter tone.

I walked over to her, putting my elbows on the back of the chair, leaning down, and gently kissing her on the top of the head. I needed to tell her I was here for her and didn't want to rush things.

I moaned and leaned my head against the back of the chair I was sitting in. Boy, that felt so good, given that small term of endearment I received from him. I had lacked any such deep and meaningful show of emotion in my life before.

I took that moan as a sign of encouragement from her and began running my fingers through her hair and massaging her scalp to ease the tension running through her body. I slipped my hands down further and started massaging her shoulders.

"Oh, Brazen," I breathed, "that feels so good. Keep going. No one has ever done this for me before. I feel like I've died and gone to heaven. It feels so good."

"Sure, I'll do anything you want, Gorgeous. I will spoil you like no one ever has done for you. I will spoil you for every other man in this world that you will only want me, Baby."

"Is that a promise, Handsome?"

"It is. I never break my promises, I assure you." I dug my fingers in a bit deeper, trying to get the knots out of her shoulders. "Mo and I will take the other ladies to Sherry's shelter after breakfast. I'm hoping you will choose to stay here with me. However, I won't force you to. If you feel that you want to go and be with the others to get help and support at the shelter, I won't stop you."

"I was thinking I want to go with the other girls to the shelter. I feel that I need time to get myself back in order. But now I'm not so sure. Especially when I have my own personal masseuse. I don't want to let you go. You're so good at this, handsome. Please don't stop. It felt like heaven, though it pained me when he ground down on the tough knots on my shoulders. It still felt good."

"Thank you for trusting me, Christa. I feel honored that you chose to stay here with me. I won't force you to do anything you don't want. You can take all the time you need. I will drive you there if you want to attend any of Sherry's counseling classes. Or if you wish to do nothing and stay here, that's fine too. I won't coerce or force you to do anything you don't want to do."

"Thank you, Brazen. I'll stay with you. I feel like I'm falling for you, and I don't know why. But I'll listen to my gut, which says you're trustworthy, and my place is to be here with you."

I leaned down and kissed her on the cheek, getting more daring and pushing my luck. "Thank you for trusting me, Gorgeous. I feel the bond, too. I think we were soul mates in a past life. I know I keep pushing that proclamation, but I feel it in me, and it feels like we have found each other again in this life." I slapped the side of her shoulders. "Sorry baby, I better help sort out the ladies for their trip to Sherry's. The only woman who won't join the others at the refuge is Gina, the unconscious lady. Doc had to transport her to the hospital due to her overwhelming injuries. Some of her injuries were internal, and she needed a place with the facilities to help her. However, when she's recovered from her injuries and discharged from the hospital, I've arranged for her to be with the other ladies at the refuge. "

"Awww, that's sad. I was worried about her. I thought she might have been dead at the time. I'm glad she's in the right place and receiving the treatment she needs, and will get to join the others later. Okay. I will come with you for the ride and wish them goodbye and all the best for their future. I hope we all stay in touch if that's what they want. Maybe they don't want to. It might bring back bad memories. I'm glad I've found my future, and I can't believe everything has happened to me." I put my book down on the side table to read later. I stood up and followed Brazen to the dining room, where the other girls were still sitting talking. It was great to see them happy in their own way, even though they had been through a lot.

Chapter Ten – Brazen & Christa

I trotted down the stairs, with Christa following close behind. I wandered into the kitchen, still buzzing with chatter among the ladies. "Hey ladies, I don't want to rush you. But we do need to get over to Sherry's. Then we give Sherry enough time to get you all registered and settled in your new accommodation and anything else you may need for your stay with her. If you still need to eat or drink more, feel free to carry on as you are. I'm not stopping you from filling yourselves with as much food as you need. But I must stress that we must leave here by ten a.m. I'll leave you to it for now and come back to sort everything out shortly for you to be ready to leave by ten.

I turned to leave and nearly bumped into Christa close behind me. "Oops, I'm sorry, Gorgeous. I forgot you were behind me. Do you want to follow me and help sort out your future in my office?" I enquired, raising my eyebrows in the hope that she would.

"Sure, I'd love to. Lead the way..." I gestured to him.

I went ahead and felt her following me to my office. I could feel the laser points of her eyes on my back and my body shivering and getting goosebumps with her close proximity to me. When we got there, I sat behind my desk and pointed to the chair in front of my desk, gesturing for her to sit. "Have you decided what you want to do yet, Baby?"

"Yeah! If the offer is still open for debate, I will stay with you and give whatever this is a chance. Also, if you want me to be here."

"No question about it, Baby. I do want you to be here with me and by my side. I got up from my desk, rushing around my desk. I pulled her out of the chair and into my arms, hugging her tight and never wanting to let go of her again in case she disappeared. I felt relieved when I felt her arms come up and hold me tight around the waist, sealing the deal in my book. I stood back, smiling at her. "Thanks, baby. I know you won't regret this decision. I'll never hurt you and will do anything for you. I better let Valeria realize she needs to arrange some bags for the ladies to pack their small stuff to take to Sherry's shelter. I use the term shelter loosely.

You will see when we get to Sherry's place. It's a substantial three-story house that she uses. They will have everything they need there. Plus, she will help set them up for the future in housing and find employment if they so desire." I returned to sit at my desk, grabbed my cell phone, and dialed Valeria's number. "Hi, it's me, Valeria. Can you arrange for some bags to be put in the ladies' rooms so they can pack their things? Thank you," hanging up the phone.

I had a thought while Brazen was on the phone. I would run it past him to see what he thinks. "I'm glad you know this, Sherry lady. I feel overwhelmed at all she will do for the girls. She will do everything she can to take them away from the horrors they endured while in the cruel imprisonment of that Torres guy. I want to help and volunteer there if she doesn't mind. It will also give me a sense of achievement and something to fill my days. Keep me out from under your feet all day," I grinned.

I smiled "damn. It would never be an imposition being under me all day, Baby," I winked for good measure of my wicked intentions.

"You're so bad," she winked back. "But I love it." I think we are going to fit together very well together, babe. I know I can trust you."

"All I want is for you to be mine, baby. All in your own good time, of course. I don't want to rush you and ruin it all. Come here, baby, and sit on my lap." I moved my chair back and patted my lap. I smiled when she got up from the chair she was sitting in and wandered over to me behind the desk.

When she reached me, I grabbed her hand, squeezing it trying to reassure her that I was no threat to her. I pull her down on my lap and kiss her on the forehead. "This is nice. I could get used to all this with you every day while I try to work," I grinned.

"I love forehead kisses, Brazen. They're so nice and reassuring." I lean up and start giving him small kisses along his jawline.

"Mmmm, that feels nice, gorgeous. Don't stop..." when I felt her stop at my comment. I hugged her tight, and then she carried on. I run my fingers up and down her spine. I was in heaven when she hid her face in my neck. I begin to run my fingers through her hair. "You gonna get shy on me now, baby?"

"Maybe," she whispered on my neck.

"Hey! I get it; this is all new. We'll take things slow, but there's no need to be shy around me, okay? Be yourself. I want to be here for you. I will help you heal and repair yourself so you're back to what you once were. Before Torres gets you back in his miserable clutches, I will ensure he pays for it and won't let him get anywhere near you again. I'm sorry to bring him up and bring back your bad memories. I only want you to know I will protect you, and no other man will get near you. They will have to go through me first. Now we need to go and get these other ladies ready to transport over to Sherry's place. Do you want to say your farewells to them? You're welcome to come along with us too if you want to meet Sherry and see where the other girls are going and that they will be safe."

"Yeah. I'd like that. I didn't spend much time with them before you rescued us. But it will bring me peace to know they are safe and have somewhere where they will be cared for and looked after. Sherry sounds amazing, and I would love to meet her. Plus, sound her out and see if she will accept me as a volunteer there."

"I'm sure she will love all the help you can give. Even I can see you're a warm, compassionate person. I'll warn you when you do go. I will be the one driving you there and picking you up. I want to keep you safe, my precious girl."

"Thank you. Now you're making me blush. No one had ever called me their precious girl before," I hated to admit, but I loved the sound of it.

"Well, they have now, and I'm glad I was the first. Cos, you mean that much to me, Baby. Now come on, let's go, or Sherry will wonder what happened to us if we're late." I lifted her off my lap, standing on the floor beside me. I was missing her heat already and felt a loss I couldn't explain.

Chapter Eleven – Brazen & Christa

I grab her hand and pull her behind me on our way to the dining room to see if the ladies are ready for us to leave for Sherry's place. I'm willing to give them some prompting if they're not yet prepared. I would let them stay longer, but I feel they would be better off staying with Sherry, giving them all the help, support, and comforts they need that I'm unable to here. "How are we going, ladies? Are you all ready to go to Sherry's, or do you need a bit longer to get your things together?"

They spoke simultaneously, so I couldn't understand what they were saying. But I think they said they were ready to leave. Since their next move was to retrieve their bags, they had left over by the side of the dining room wall.

Just then, Mo arrived, saying, "Please follow me, ladies, your chariot awaits," bowing and smiling at the ladies. He walked towards the front door, escorting the ladies to our van waiting out the front.

I grinned in amazement. I had never seen this calm and reassuring mode Mo had going here for the ladies. "Are you ready to go, gorgeous? Do you still want to come to Sherry's place with us?"

"Of course I do. I wouldn't miss it for the world, baby. I didn't know the ladies for long or very well. Under different circumstances, we might be friends or not, who knows. But we shared a traumatizing experience, and our past will forever link us. Yes, I'm as ready as I will ever be." I linked my arm around Brazen's elbow while he led me out to the van and helped me up the step into the van. I sat down, and he slammed the door shut behind me. Then Mo and Brazen entered the front, and we drove the short drive to Sherry's house.

It was an uneventful twenty-minute ride to Sherry's house. It made me smile when I heard them oohing and aahing in surprise from the back when they spotted the house from the driveway. Sherry had inherited her family mansion and turned it into a refuge to help women escape domestic violence and human trafficking. When we arrived at the house's entrance, Mo parked our van. I spotted Sherry coming out before we even had a chance to get out.

Sherry came out and was walking down the steps. She came over to the window I had wound down, smiling and greeting us, "Hello. How are my two favorite men in the world?" to Mo and myself.

"Morning, Sherry," we both responded to her. "We're good. We have some lovely new ladies for you to look after in the back of the van." I opened my door and got out when Sherry stepped back, allowing me to do so. I went over, opening the side door and enabling the ladies to exit. "Just leave your bags, ladies. Mo and I will bring them in for you. You follow Sherry, and we'll follow behind with your bags." I smiled.

"Thank you, Brazen and Mo," they chorused.

"No problem, ladies. It's been a pleasure. Sorry, we had to meet under these circumstances. However, we like to help any ladies in distress that we find during work and look after them, especially when they are as well-behaved as yourselves." I smiled.

I watched them file in after Sherry while opening the back of the van and filling Mo's arms with bags before bringing the rest in myself. I called out to Sherry, taking the ladies into the processing room. We'll leave the ladies' bags at the top of the stairs for you to sort through later. We'll be on our way and leave you in peace now."

"Thanks, Brazen," she called out. "I'll ring you later tonight when I have some spare time and let you know how we went today."

"No worries, I'll talk to you then," tipping my chin in her direction. I followed Mo up the first flight of stairs, where we deposited the bags near the wall out of the way. We hurried back down the stairs to the van. I hopped in the back next to my girl Christa while Mo got in the driver's side to drive us home.

"I can't believe we're finally alone now, Gorgeous," I whispered in her ear. I smiled when I felt her shiver with my musings. "Are you okay,

Baby? I don't want to scare you away. Or are you shivering because you're cold? Do you need my jacket?"

"Yeah, I'm good, Baby," while absentmindedly wringing my hands together. "It made me feel I don't know all tingly inside. Something I have never felt for anyone before."

"I'm glad I made you feel tingly inside Gorgeous. I feel so much for you. More than I probably should, but I feel such a connection between us. I can't even explain how or why. I don't want to rush you either. I want to take things slowly with you. I feel so much for you."

"I know, handsome. I wish I knew what this was, too. I should fear you after all I have been through. But it's the complete opposite. I'm feeling things for you that I maybe shouldn't this soon after meeting you. I wish I could explain it, but I can't." I looked up from my hands, staring into his eyes. God, those beautiful blue eyes of his draw me in, and I find myself losing myself in them. I'm maybe even drowning in those deep blue pools. "I think I feel everything you feel, and I don't know or understand why," I said honestly while wondering what this was, whether I should even feel this, or if I had Stockholm syndrome. I don't think it's that maybe if I fell for that other asshole Torres. But not this charming, sweet man sitting beside me. He had rescued me from a fate unknown but no doubt a horrific one at the hands of Torres.

"Aww baby, I get you." I cupped her cheeks with my hands, gently kissing the tip of her nose. "Come on, let's get you home and settled in your room. However, you are most welcome to share my room and bed if I'm not rushing you. I might be selfish only thinking of myself here," I smirked.

I pull away, look at him, and sigh... this man, what he does to me while I slowly melt inside. I may be rushing things here, but what the hell? You only live once, and I trust this man wholeheartedly. I lean over and kiss him on the cheek, even scaring myself. *Oh shit, did I do that?* My eyes widened in terror.

Oh, fuck did she just kiss me? Even I couldn't believe it. Judging by the horrified expression on her face, she scared herself too. I don't think she can quite believe she kissed me, either. "Well, thank you, gorgeous. I enjoyed that. Did you scare yourself, too, judging by the look on your face? However, feel free to kiss me more often if you like. I won't be doing any complaining."

All I could do was blush and nod in agreement at him. I had even stunned myself speechless.

I reached over and grabbed her cheeks with my hands and gently kissed her on the lips. I smiled when I felt her melt into the kiss and moan against my lips. I licked her bottom lip and gained entry when she parted her luscious, ruby lips to let me in. She tasted sweet as sugar when I tasted her. Then, when I leaned further into the kiss, we began battling tongues against each other. I groaned when I could feel my cock getting hard and pressing against the seam in my jeans. I was soon brought back to earth with a throat clearing from the front seat. *Fuck, I forgot about Mo, up there in the front driving. What on earth was I thinking?*

"Everything okay back there?" I inquired. I was more concerned for Christa, worried that Brazen might be taking advantage of her in his lust. I needed to check and ensure she was okay with what Brazen was doing.

"Silence in the cheap seats, Mo," I bit back. "Sorry, I forgot where we were when I got lost in the moment. You'll be happy to note I shall restrain myself now." Then I leaned back in my seat, pulling Christa close to my side for the rest of the journey back home.

"Okay, pal, keep your hat on. There's no need to snap at me there; I'm just calling it like it is. I was more concerned for Christa and that you may be moving too fast for her here, Buddy."

"Sorry for biting at you, Mo. I shouldn't have lost it with you. I'm glad you had Christa's best interests at heart because I did get carried away and didn't have her best interests at heart."

"Apology accepted," I nodded.

When we were close to his house, I leaned over and whispered in Brazen's ear, "I trust you and will always choose you. I've been thinking, and if the offer is still open, I'm happy to share your room and bed."

I couldn't stop the smile beaming across my face, "of course it is, my sweet girl. The offer will always be open even if you change your mind at the last moment. I shall respect your decision even if you change your mind. I don't want to rush you and spoil things between us. I want to take things slowly and make them right. I would do anything for you, my gorgeous girl. You're the only one that matters here for me," giving her hand a tight squeeze to let her know I meant what I said.

Before we knew it, Mo was turning off the main highway and pulling into the driveway of the compound, then through the security gates. He stopped in front of the main steps to let us out before he went and parked our van in the garage. I slid the door open and got out. I then put up my hand, taking Christa's hand tight in my grip and helping her down the few steps out of the van. I held her hand while brushing my thumb against the back of her hand while we ascended the stairs. Before I could put my hand on the handle and open the door, it was whipped out of my hand when Valeria opened it for us. "Well, hello there," I grinned at her. "Are you pleased to see me back, Valeria?"

"No. I mean, yes, Sir, and pleased to see Madam back too," she smiled.

I roared with laughter. "I know what you mean. I'm pleased she decided to stay with us, too."

I walked us through the door, informing Valeria, "we are not to be disturbed, okay? We then walked through the foyer and ascended the stairs toward my bedroom.

Chapter Twelve – Brazen & Christa

We entered my bedroom, and I kicked the door shut behind us. I walked her over to the bed before picking her up. I stared into those eyes of hers made of melted gold, melting me inside while I sat next to her on the bed. I leant down, removing her shoes, swinging her legs up onto the bed. Next, I shucked my boots off, closely followed by my socks, and leaped into bed beside her. I pulled the blankets over us and wrapped my arm around her waist.

I began getting the fluttering of butterflies in my belly when he wrapped his hand around my waist. "I can see what you're up to, and you know what you're doing," I squinted my eyes while looking at him.

"Who me?" clutching my hand to my chest, feigning innocence. "You've hurt my feelings now, Gorgeous" I pouted, trying not to smile, but I couldn't help myself. It burst forth into laughter.

"You faker you," I told him, slapping him on the chest with my hand.

This made me turn on my side, grabbing and pulling her closer. "Only kidding. I apologize. I feel so comfortable with you already, Gorgeous."

"I feel you, baby. I can feel the connection between us, too even though I maybe shouldn't under the circumstances. My gut says to trust you. Therefore, I am." I gave him a gentle squeeze back. I felt nervous about all these emotions that felt like they were colliding, causing me to feel overwhelmed. I felt comfortable lying against his warm body with my head resting on his shoulder. I didn't ever want to leave.

"This feels nice," I said while running my fingers through her long, silky hair.

"Mmmm... it does, I wish. I could stay here forever," I murmured.

"You can," I whispered to her. "Let's get some more sleep, Baby. Then we'll get up later and do something nice together later."

"Yeah! I'm nearly there with your hottie body warming me up here and making me feel comfortable enough to sleep."

I grinned like an idiot at her. I was smitten. "Back at you gorgeous. How did I get so lucky?" I mused. No response. I looked down at her, and she was sound asleep. I followed shortly behind.

I awoke with a start. I was so hot and couldn't move. My handsome man hugged me tight to his body, and I was also entangled in the sheets. No wonder I was hot. I tried to move without waking him, but I was unsuccessful.

"What's wrong? Is everything okay, my gorgeous girl?" I awoke panicking that something was wrong with her panic to get out of bed.

"No, it's all good. I'm hot, and I only need to pee. Honest..."

"Well, I better let you go then. I better not hold you up. Don't be long. I miss you already, baby" watching her while she sashayed to the ensuite bathroom. I groaned to myself. I can't wait till I feel myself balls deep inside her. I want and need her so badly. When she finished and came out of the bathroom, I was sitting on the side of the bed. "Come here, baby" I pouted, holding my arms out to wrap them around her hips. I looked up, ready to kiss her.

She leaned down and gave me a small peck on the lips. "Do you mind if I shower to freshen up and then have lunch? I'm starting to feel hungry."

"Sure Baby, you can treat this house as your own now. You can go anywhere and help yourself to anything you need or want here. I only ask if I'm in my office with the door closed. Please knock first. Then wait for me to tell you to enter or tell you to come back later if I can't be disturbed. Let's go shopping later this afternoon and get you a new wardrobe."

"Thank you, baby. It might take me some getting used to wandering around your...

"Ahem, excuse me, Baby, it's our house now. Remember that, okay?" I corrected her.

"Of course, if you're sure handsome. That's not what I'm like, Baby. I'm not a gold digger. I wouldn't do that. I do have some manners. I would love to go shopping with you. Now, if you will excuse me, I'll have my shower... We better add toiletries and other personal items to the list, Handsome." I smirked at my cheek, asking for more things on his dime.

"Anything and everything you need or would like; you shall have Gorgeous. What about your family? Do you want to contact anyone and let them know that you're safe?" I inquired.

"No, not really. I mean, I have my dad. But we weren't close, and he kept me away from home. He kept me traveling once I finished college. He gave me free rein to spend his money once my mom and brother were gone. I felt like a pain in his butt being around the house, especially when he had a woman spend the night. Maybe one day I might. But I don't feel the need to contact him now. He probably doesn't even know I'm missing. Though maybe he might when I'm not spending his money," I grimaced with a pained laugh.

"Hey, whenever you feel ready, just let me know. I'll be there with you every step of the way whenever you contact your dad. Sorry, he made you feel like that. But I'll always be here for you. Please know that" I tried to reassure her.

"I know handsome. Thank you for all that you're doing for me. Now, if you'll please excuse me, I'll go have my shower." I didn't want to talk about my father anymore. It pained me to do so for some reason.

"Okay," slapping her on the ass when she walked past me. "If you need help scrubbing your back, I'm there." I winked when she looked back at me.

"I'm good, thanks. I'm sure I can do my own back," she grinned. "Maybe another time," I winked at him.

"Alrighty then. I'll see if I can find some of my clothes to fit you until we can go shopping." I went to my armoire and found her a T-shirt and a pair of drawstring gym shorts. She could at least pull them tight to keep them up. Unfortunately, she would be panty and braless since they weren't part of my wardrobe. I heard the shower turn on and the door open and then close. I was so tempted to go in there and give her a hand. But I held myself back. I wanted to take things slowly with Christa since she meant a lot to me, and I didn't want to stuff this relationship in any way. I wanted her to be mine for life. I wondered if I should call her bluff and scrub her back in that shower.

Yep, I convinced myself to do it. You need a shower too; let's conserve water is my excuse to have ready. Well, I have to convince myself of that anyway. I got up while stripping my clothes off on the way to the bathroom. I tossed my shirt aside. I opened the door and removed my jeans and boxer shorts. I opened the door of the shower and snuck in behind her.

"What took you so long, handsome?" she giggled.

Damnit, I'm glad I came in here now, I thought to myself. "Hmmm, I thought of everything I could do to you in this shower when you were gone." I leaned down, kissed her on the side of her neck, and slowly kissed my way up to her lips. I turned her head around and kissed the edge of her mouth, then licked my tongue along her bottom lip, hoping she would grant me entry. I felt my cock harden when she breathed out a moan. I snuck my tongue in, taking full advantage of that moan. I nipped her tongue before tasting her mouth tasting like bubble gum from her lip gloss. "Mmmm, you taste delicious, baby. Now I need to taste the rest of you..."

I kissed down her chest to her nice set of tits, first lathing one nipple, then the other got some attention too. I kissed down her belly, licking around her navel where some water had collected. I bent down on my knees and spread her legs to taste her pussy and tease her clit. I ran my tongue along her seam and began licking and tasting her pussy while running my thumb across, teasing her clit.

I smiled when I made her moan with all the attention I was giving her. God, she tasted damn good too. I wouldn't ever be able to get enough of her. I was going to lick her and make her cum all over me before I fucked that tight juicy pussy of hers. I licked her from her pussy down her clit and nibbled and sucked on her clit. I felt her legs begin to shake as I carried on licking her toward that end goal. I gripped her hips tight; I didn't want her to fall. I licked down to her pussy, licking her deep while I rubbed my thumb against her clit until she came with a moan, and I felt the rush of her release in my mouth. "Mmmm... you taste very delicious, baby."

I stood up with great effort since my cock was rock hard now. I decided to wash her hair. I grabbed the shampoo, washing her hair. I was pleased with my job, judging by her moans of delight while I massaged her head; it appeared she did, too. I washed her shampoo out before adding the conditioner. Once I washed the conditioner, I grabbed the facecloth and washed her body. "Let's go back to bed and finish now, baby," I whispered in her ear.

"Hey, that's not fair. Let me wash you first. Fair is fair. You did me. Now I get to do you." I huffed in disappointment since he seemed in a hurry to get out of the shower.

"Okay, but hurry, gorgeous. I don't know how long I will last here."

"Sure, sure, Handsome." I grabbed the shampoo and washed his hair, followed by the conditioner. Now for the fun part: washing his body. I grabbed the facecloth and soaped it with the citrus body wash. I decided to tease him. I slowly ran the facecloth down his back. I smiled to myself when he growled at me to hurry up. I rubbed the facecloth across his butt cheeks, then my finger slipped and poked in his asshole.

"Fuck Gorgeous. What are you doing to me? I almost came on the spot, then Gorgeous. Fuck, fuck, fuck."

"Sorry, not," I giggled back. I loved teasing him and carried on running the washcloth down both legs. "Okay, turn around now so I can do your front, Handsome." Well, look at that when he turned around, his cock bouncing around in my face. I washed his legs, dropping the cloth. I placed my hands on his thighs, licked his balls, and then I sucked his balls into my mouth. Before popping off, telling him, "Mmmm... my handsome man is such a mouthful of blue balls. Now I will fill my mouth with that gorgeous cock." I stared with desire at his hard veiny cock twitching and twisting around in front of my eyes. I licked the tip across her slit. "Mmmm, yummy baby." I sucked his cock in my mouth, licking and twisting my tongue around his hard length. I sucked him more, trying not to gag on his long length. I ran my finger along his balls, taking him by surprise again when I jabbed my finger in his ass again.

"Fuck" this wasn't happening. I pulled out of her mouth with a pop. "Baby," I sighed, leaning down and picking her up. "We are finishing this in bed, not here." I turned the shower off and opened the door, carrying her in my arms until we reached the bed and threw her down on top. I didn't care that we were still wet from the shower. I needed her, and right now, nothing would stop me. I shook my head at the large grin she had across her face. "That cheeky grin might disappear shortly when you see what I have in store for you, Gorgeous."

I pushed her thighs wide apart, staring down at her glistening wet pussy ready and waiting and wanting me to fill her. I stare down at her perky tits with her nipples in taut points, wanting some attention. God, where do I start? I slide two fingers into her wet pink pussy, watching her back arc off the bed with the intrusion. I lean down and suck her nipple, licking my tongue around and then biting down on her nipple. Which causes her to moan and push my fingers deeper into her pussy. She's so needy. "Fuck you need this, don't you, baby."

"Oh, fuck me now, please, Baby," I moaned when he put two fingers in my needy pussy and began sucking my hard nipples. I was broke for his attention. I needed him everywhere. I was aching for him so much. Nothing would relieve the want and ache as he could. I had it bad for him.

I slid my fingers out since she was so ready for me. I sucked her delicious juices from my fingers before I grabbed hold of my cock and tapped her clit. "First, I'm going to fuck you deep and hard, gorgeous. Round two, we will make slow, sweet love." I lined my cock up with her sweet pussy and rammed him home hard. "Yes..." I yelled. God, she felt so good with her tight hot little pussy gripping my cock tight.

"Oooh," I moaned. It felt so good. I could feel the thick vein in his cock pulsing hard, vibrating against the sensitive walls of my pussy. I wanted to grip his cock hard and never let him go. I felt a loss when he pulled out again.

"Yes... baby," pulling back before I rammed him home deep and hard within her once again. I stilled, letting her pussy walls grip me hard, trying hard to squeeze an orgasm out of me. The way her walls were pulsing while gripping my cock, it wasn't going to take long before I was filling her full of my cum. "Oh, yessss," when her tight pussy walls squeezed my cock. I needed to release my load and fill her full. Once more, she gripped my cock, and my balls tightened, and I released my load in her needy pussy. I collapsed on top of her for a minute or two before pulling out of her and collapsing beside her. Once I had caught my breath, I leaned my head on my hand, watching my cum slowly leaking out of her pussy. I couldn't resist the temptation and wiped the leaking cum up with my finger telling her, "open wide and suck my finger, clean baby." I felt myself getting hard again while she dutifully sucked my finger clean.

"Mmmm, delicious baby," I told him while busy sucking his finger and tasting us both. It felt like such a fantastic experience—something I had never done before. I felt so loved when he grabbed me in his arms, rolling over and taking me with him. He held me tight in his arms, where I could feel and hear his heart beating in his chest. I could feel his love for me. I nearly had tears come to my eyes. I had never had someone love me so much before. I slowly drifted back to sleep with the steady pounding of his heart in my ear.

Chapter Thirteen – Brazen & Christa

I woke with a start. It must have been late in the afternoon because the light in the bedroom was beginning to fade with the sun setting. I slapped her on the ass "come on, baby—time to wake up. We've nearly slept the day away. Everyone will be wondering what happened to us."

"Ugh! Do we have to? I was enjoying that dream and everything I was doing to you," I sighed. I rolled over in his direction but had not yet opened my eyes. What is he thinking? It's so lovely here, snuggled up in his warm bed. I didn't ever want to leave. I was loving it here. It felt so luxurious, especially after having to sleep on a cold basement floor for goodness knows how long. "Come back in here with me, handsome," I asked him while patting the mattress beside me, waiting for him to join me.

"I'm sorry, Gorgeous. I know it's too comfy in there. Believe I would join you, but we might never leave if I get in there, then I will keep you busy all night long in there. But it is nearly dinner time. You do need to eat, and so do I. Sadly, after dinner, I will need to go and do some work that requires finishing off in my office." I sat on the bed, dragging her in my arms, holding her close while running my fingers through her long, silky hair. I placed a gentle kiss on top of her head. "I'll have to give you one of my shirts to wear. I'm sorry about that love. We never did get out on our shopping trip, did we? Ah well, tomorrow is another day." I walked over to the armoire, pulled out a blue button-down shirt, and threw it over to her sitting in bed.

"Yeah, thanks handsome." I caught it and pulled it close to me. I loved the thought of wearing one of his t-shirts, and I could feel even closer to him. I sniffed the collar to smell his woodsy leather scent lingering on his shirt, causing me to sigh. I dragged myself away from sniffing his shirt, which seemed to be causing him great amusement. I put it on and buttoned up the shirt. "Do you have some socks, too handsome, so I don't get cold feet on the floors? I don't have shoes either?"

"Of course," shaking my head in amusement after watching her sniff my shirt. This was the first time I had seen someone do that, but anyway, I digress. I wandered back to the armoire and found a short pair of socks; although they would still be too big for her, they might fit her better. I threw them over. "Maybe don't sniff those either. Gorgeous, you might choke on them even if they are clean." I laughed in amusement at her antics.

"Are you making fun of me, handsome?" I raised an accusing eyebrow at him.

"Who me?" pointing to my chest. "Never gorgeous," I winked before leaning down and kissing her on the forehead. "Now come on." I picked up the socks I had tossed. I lifted one silky long leg and put one sock on her delicate foot. I placed it gently down and then picked up her other leg, putting the other sock on. I grabbed her by the hands, pulling her up off the bed. "Now let's go downstairs and eat, woman," leading her out of the bedroom and down the stairs.

"Ooh, you going all caveman on me, Braze?"

"Of course. I must warn you that some guys usually hang around for food, especially if we have a meeting. Therefore, don't let them put you off. They'll make you welcome and might give you some shit but ignore them or give as good as you get. Your choice baby. You're mine now baby, and you're here to stay. They'll know to leave you alone."

"Okay, got it, handsome. I might be a bit shy initially since I don't know them. Plus, I'm not good at remembering names. I hope they forgive me if I mistake or forget their names."

I pulled her hand up, kissing her knuckles. "They will or will have to deal with me," I winked. I gathered, judging by the noise from the kitchen. I could tell a few of the men had decided to stay for a meal.

Chapter Fourteen – Brazen & Christa (Three months later)

I decided to have a special night for my darling Christa when I found out it was her twenty-fifth birthday the following Saturday. I had decided to surprise her and propose. I hope she will accept me as her man for the rest of our lives. I had arranged to take her to the Surf and Turf restaurant in the next town in style. I had made a reservation at the restaurant, and we would go in style in a Hummer limousine I had hired from one of my acquaintances who owes me a favor. It was going to be only the best for my baby. I was bouncing around with excitement. I couldn't contain my excitement at everything I had planned. I pulled my credit card out of my wallet and searched for Christa so she could go and buy herself a lovely dress for our special night out.

I found her in the kitchen having a coffee. "Hey, baby. I would like you to do something for me."

"Sure. What would you like me to do for you, handsome.?"

"Here's my credit card. Will you go and buy yourself a special dress and matching shoes? I will take you out next Saturday to celebrate your birthday." I smiled, cupping her cheek with my hand, leaning down, and kissing her forehead.

"Oh gosh! I have never had anything do that for me before and take me out on my birthday." I blushed with excitement. "I've only celebrated by myself or with my friends, never with a special man. My father never seemed to bother either..." I could feel tears pricking my eyes. No, not now...

"Well, you're special to me, Baby, and I like to spoil what's mine. I'm glad I will be giving you another first in your life. I will spoil you like you have never been before, baby. I hope you enjoy everything I have planned for you." I could hardly wait for the following weekend to spoil her and see the reactions on her face.

I downed the rest of the coffee left in my cup. "I guess I better get to the mall and find myself a dress and shoes to spoil my boyfriend. I stood up and held my hand out. "you better give me the SUV keys, handsome. I don't anticipate walking to the mall." I smiled when he pulled them out of his pocket and dropped them in my hand. He's always prepared like he knows what I want before I do. "Thanks, baby," I grabbed him by the front of his shirt, pulling him in close for a deep kiss on the lips.

"I might have to do this more often if I'm gonna get thanked like this, my gorgeous girl," I grinned. I slapped her on the ass, smiling when I made her squeal. "Come on, get outta here and hit the mall, my gorgeous girl." I put my finger on my chin, pretending to be deep in thought, "maybe you should get some sexy lingerie to surprise me with, too, while you're at it," I winked.

"Got it," I smiled, walking out of the kitchen and out to the front door. I walked to the SUV and got in, shaking my head at how lucky I was now. I started the car and headed down the driveway after programming the closest mall in the GPS since I wasn't familiar with the area. I smiled at Beans guarding the front gate. I thanked him when he waved at me after opening the gate, allowing me to leave. I had a pleasant drive into town and quickly found a parking place. I hopped out and walked in through in the entry, deciding which shop to hit first. I decided on the lingerie shop I saw up ahead, smiling secretly. I was going to go overboard in here; I knew it. I browsed through the racks and found a sexy red bustier with black diamantes dotted throughout the lace with matching panties and suspenders. I took them into the changing room to try them on, and they fit perfectly. I told the sales lady when I took them over to where she stood at the counter, "I'll take these, thank you. I also want to get some stockings, too, but I'm not sure what color to pick to go with them. Do you think red, white, or black ones?"

"Entirely up to you, ma'am. But I would go with either the red or white."

"Hmmm," I pondered. "I might go with the red then," after picturing a red dress I hoped to find in my mind since I planned to go all out in my favorite color, red. I watched her while she picked a red pair from behind the counter to add to my purchases.

"Will that be all, ma'am, or do you need help with anything else?"

"No, that's all for now; thank you so much for all your help," I smiled, pleased with my purchases. I couldn't wait to see Brazen's face when he saw them. I waited while she rang them up and handed them over in a shopping bag after ringing up the credit card to pay for them. "Thank you," and turned to head out to the door.

"You're welcome, ma'am. I hope to see you back another time," she smiled.

"I'm sure I will," I grinned. Now, where to go next? I headed to the information board to see which dress shops they had in the mall. Hmmm... That one French Kiss catches my imagination. That one sounds like an excellent place to start, I thought to myself. I headed toward the French Kiss Boutique to see what wonders they had to offer. Hoping that they had what I was looking for. I didn't mind shopping, but I wouldn't say I liked it if I had to stroll around many shops to find what I was looking for.

I found their store, and it looked promising from the window display. I entered the store, and the clerk welcomed me.

Good afternoon, madam. Welcome to the French Kiss Boutique. Can I help you, or would you prefer to browse?"

"I might browse for now. If I find what I'm looking for, I'll let you know so I can try it on."

"Most certainly. Feel free to see me if we don't have your size on the rack. We may have more sizes available out the back."

"Thank you," I smiled at the assistant. I spotted some red dresses near the back of the store and headed towards them. I had decided I was going to pick a red dress. I saw a beautiful one that had a fitted bodice sleeveless on one shoulder and the other shoulder a strap over the ruched bodice. When I tried it on, the pleated skirt on the dress fell to mid-calf, and it had a thigh-high split on the left side. I decided this was the dress. I was going to drive Brazen wild wearing it. I heard the assistant fussing around outside the door. I opened the door to ask her opinion on the dress. "How does this look on me?" I asked.

"Oh my gosh, ma'am. You look stunning, and red is certainly your color, ma'am. It suits you and that dress on you. Wow," she beamed. "Your man will fall at your feet when he sees you in this dress.".

"Thank you, that was the look I was going for. It looks like I nailed it on the first try. I'll take it." I turned and returned to the changing room to put my clothes on and took the dress out to the front counter once I was dressed. "Is there a shoe store in the mall you could recommend? I will need some shoes to go with the dress next."

"Certainly, ma'am. Infinity Shoe store has a great range of high-end shoes. Plus, they also sell purses if you're looking for one of those too." I ran the credit card and bagged up the dress, handing it to my customer. "Pleasure doing business with you, ma'am, and hope we see you again."

"Thank you, and I certainly will. You have a great range and pleasant customer service." I grabbed the bag from the assistant and searched for the store she had recommended. Luckily for me, I didn't have far to go. It was only three stores down from the dress shop. I entered the store and was pleasantly surprised at the range they had. I picked out a pair of black stiletto strappy shoes to go with my red dress. I also found a small red clutch purse to go with my dress. My outfit for the night was now complete. Once my purchase had been paid for and bagged up, I left the store. It was hungry and thirsty work this shopping lark. I searched for a café next to have a coffee and a bite to eat.

I was pleased to find one and sat down to take a load off my feet. I put my purchases on the seat next to me. I picked up the menu off the table, browsing it to see what I felt like eating. I chose a bagel with smoked salmon, cream cheese, and coffee. I gave my order to the server when she came around to take my order. I retrieved my phone out of my purse to see if I had any missed calls or messages. I smiled to see I had a text from Brazen.

'**Miss you, baby. I hope you're having fun.**

I smiled to myself at his text. I responded, '**Miss you heaps too. I hope I haven't spent too much.** ☺'

Brazen '**Never. Spend all you like. I can afford it $$$** ☺'

He always makes me smile at this man. I don't know what I would ever do without him now. He had found his way into my heart and was never going to leave, that was for sure. My server returned and placed my food in front of me.

"I'll be right back with your coffee, ma'am."

"Thank you," I smiled in return. I soon scoffed down my bagel. It was so delicious, and I appeared hungrier than I realized. I took my time over coffee, reading a book on my phone app. I decided to have another coffee and stay seated a bit longer. I needed a lovely, lazy morning and enjoyed the peace and quiet. Previously, I had never had anywhere to settle since I was always traveling to keep out of my father's hair. Sometimes, it could get hectic at Brazen's place with all the other guys around the house. Once I was done, I picked my purchases up, returned to my car in the car park, and drove back home to my man.

When I got home, he was waiting at the front door for me. I shook my head, smiling. "You miss me that bad, huh?" I grinned, getting out of the car. "You couldn't even wait for me to get inside."

"Yeah, I did. I wanna see what you brought, gorgeous." I grabbed her around the waist and kissed her on the cheek. I tried to peek in her bags, but she wasn't having it and whipped them away so I couldn't see anything.

"Uh, no Handsome. You won't see these babies until next Saturday when we go out. I want to surprise you on the night. I will make sure I hide them well, too. I don't want you to be tempted to look for them and spoil my surprise." I laughed at the look on his face, like a child whose piece of candy had been snatched away from them.

"Awww baby. You know me so well," I laughed. "Now I can't wait for next Saturday night. I've got a few surprises for you, too," I winked.

"Well, we'll be even then, won't we?" I wrapped my free arm around his waist, swinging around him and walking inside. While I left Brazen in the kitchen, I headed upstairs to find somewhere to hide my purchases. I decided anywhere in plain view was too obvious—probably not a good idea. I didn't know where else in the house to hide my purchases. I hid them under the bed, the only place I could think of for now. At least they were still wrapped in their packaging. I hoped this would be one place Brazen would check for, at least. That task out the way, I went back downstairs to join him in the kitchen.

Chapter Fifteen – Brazen & Christa

Before I knew it, Saturday had arrived, and her birthday was here. When she finally woke up, she got her first birthday present. I had been waiting patiently for a while, watching her sleep, willing her to wake up so I could get rid of my morning wood. I flung the blankets back and lifted her nightie. I knelt between her legs and set her legs over my shoulders. Then I delved into her sweet pussy, licking her delicious juices and tormenting the hell out of her clit until she came while screaming the house down while she did it. Yep, I think everyone knew what we just did now. If they weren't awake before, they sure would be now. I looked up and grinned, my chin wet with her luscious juices, sating my thirst. "Well, Happy Birthday. I hope you enjoyed your gift. Now that's my thirst taken care of, baby. Now, I need to get rid of this morning wood I'm sprouting here. I know it's your birthday. I'm sorry, but not sorry that I'm taking something for myself while I'm at it. I will take all the credit for it. I slowly entered her tight hot wet pussy, causing her to groan, followed by a moan breaking free from my mouth. She felt fucking amazing wrapped around my hard cock.

"Fuck Brazen, how come you always know what to do. Right there, please. Don't stop, please, I'm begging you. It feels so delicious, and I'm going to cum any moment again." I could feel the pleasure building up again. I don't know how this man did it, but he did.

"Mmmm... I know, Babe, and I will be cumming with you. He's not going to last much longer. He knows where home is and enjoys the pleasure it gives him. Fuccck..." when her pussy gripped my cock hard when she came and took me with her. I felt my cum spurt deep inside her. There was so much I didn't think I would ever stop. One final pump inside her, and I collapsed on top of her before rolling off onto my side of the bed. "Wow, Baby," I muttered, throwing my left arm across my chest.

When I recovered and regained my strength, I reached over to my nightstand. I grabbed my birthday gift out of the top drawer for her. "Happy Birthday Baby. I hope you enjoy the evening I have planned for us." I kissed her deeply on the lips and gave her my present.

"Thank you, Baby. I wonder what it is," I grinned. Already knowing it was a piece of jewelry from the size of the box. I couldn't contain myself with the excitement of wondering what the box contained. I may have ripped the gift wrap and ribbon off. I was so excited I couldn't get it open fast enough.

"Settle down, Baby," I laughed. "It won't disappear if you take your time opening it."

"I know I'm just excited. I have never had someone give me any jewelry before. My parents did, but that's not the same as something from my handsome and sexy man." I gasped when peeking inside the wrapping and saw the beige velvet box. I slowly lifted the lid, trying to look, squinting with one eye to see if I could see what was inside. I gasped, and my heart skipped a beat when I lifted the top completely open. "Oh my god, Brazen this must have cost you a small fortune. Inside was a Bulgari ruby and diamond necklace and a matching watch. Oh god, Brazen why did you spend so much on me?" Tears rolled down my cheeks at this special gift of love from Brazen. It was worth too much money. I was sure I would be too scared to wear them in public.

"Hey Baby, look at me," grabbing her chin to face me. "I didn't mean to make you cry, my love. I love you so much. I can afford it and wanted to show you how much I love you and get you something special to go with the amazing dress I'm sure you brought to wear tonight. I'm so sorry. I didn't mean to make you cry on your birthday. It's just that I have never had anyone to spoil in my life before. I'm sorry if I went overboard on my gift." I felt guilty now I had made her a blubbering mess.

Gosh, why was I such a blubbering mess? "I'm sorry," I blubbered through tears. "I will cherish these for the rest of my life. I love them.

They're beautiful and unique cos you gave them to me." I threw my arms around his waist and clutched him tight, never wanting to let go. I loved this man so much. 'Thank you, Brazen. I love you so much and will never ever forget this day."

"I hope so too, Baby and I want to spoil you for the rest of our lives together, too," I assured her. I grabbed a couple of tissues on the nightstand and wiped her tears away. "I'm glad they're tears of joy and not tears of sorrow, my sweet baby girl."

"Never," she sniffed. "You always make me happy."

"Come on. Hop up, and let's go have a shower and get dressed. I'll get some breakfast for you; hopefully, that will make you feel better. Although I can't guarantee you won't get slammed against the wall in the shower and taken over again.'

"I wouldn't expect anything less." I grinned, following him into the bathroom. I shrugged my nightie off as I tossed it in the laundry hamper. True to his word when I stepped in the shower ahead of him. I found myself getting spun around and slammed against the shower wall before I knew what was happening. He lifted me, and his cock, like always, found his way home and slammed home deep and hard inside me for the second time this morning. "Oh God, Brazen you're amazing," feeling myself cumming quickly and fast with his cock in me, hitting all the right spots. Once he recovered, he placed me back down on the floor. He loved and cherished me while shampooing my hair and washing my body. When he was finished, he chuffed me out of the shower. Something about leaving him in peace while I went and got dressed. Plus, I better go downstairs and eat breakfast, where he would join me when he had finished. He was going to spoil me more. It seemed he had organized a team of people coming to spoil me. He had someone arriving at two to do my hair and makeup for our night out.

I dressed in leggings and a pink sweater for the day and went downstairs to wait for Brazen to appear and join me and have breakfast together. He joined me not long after. We enjoyed our coffee and breakfast alone since the other men must've eaten earlier and cleared out, leaving us in peace.

Chapter Sixteen – Brazen & Christa

It felt like I was bouncing around on cloud nine. I was buzzing with excitement about tonight. Not only that, but the nervous tension was also flowing through my veins at what I was doing tonight. I would propose to my gorgeous girl and make her mine for the rest of my life. I had never pictured myself doing this in my life before. I checked my suit pocket to ensure the little jewelry box was still inside. I didn't want to lose it. I hoped Christa loved the ring I had picked for her. More to the point, I expected my girl would say yes to my proposal. However, Mo assured me there was no way that girl could say no to me. She loved me too much, and even he could see that.

I heard my phone vibrate in my pocket. I pulled it out to check the message, and it was from Buzz down at the gate. He told me he had just let the limousine in the gate. Yikes, it was beginning to get real now. I gulped the lump down in my throat and went upstairs to our bedroom to see if my princess was ready to go. I knocked and opened the door when she called out...

"Come in. I'm decent," called from the bedroom. "Oh, it's you handsome. Wow, I never thought the day would come that I would see you in a suit. I can't believe how handsome you look, Babe. You should wear one more often."

I was still trying to pull my jaw off from the floor. I couldn't believe the beautiful red dress she was wearing. She looked stunning in red. I would enjoy taking that fucking thing off her incredible body later if I didn't rip it off first. Hell, if I did, she could always buy another one. "I can't believe the stunning vision before me. Gorgeous, and you're all mine. My beautiful lady..." I was sure I'd died and gone to heaven, and the vision before me was an angel sent to taunt me. "I'll try not to rip that beautiful dress off your body later tonight, though no promises. I might need you to wear it again just for me. Oh, hell if I weaken and rip the dress off you, you can go and buy another one."

"Oh, Braze, those are the most beautiful words I've ever heard in my life. Thank you." I held my arms out to embrace him and held him close, resting my head on his shoulder, smelling his delicious citrusy scent. "You better not rip this dress either. I love it, and it's my new favorite." *I can't believe he's mine*, clutching him tight and never wanting to let him go.

I gripped her tight and never wanted to let her go and touched my lips on the top of her head. "Come on, Babe it's time to go. Our ride is here. Now hurry before my cock gives in to my urges and I end up tossing you down on this bed."

I giggled at his threat. "Okay. I'm ready. I gotta grab my clutch off the nightstand." I grabbed it and then took hold of Brazen's hand. We walked down the hallway and the stairs toward the front door. When he opened the door...

I nearly burst into tears again when I saw the men outside in a line of honor on the steps. All saluted us as we walked down the stairs towards the limousine. "Thank you guys, you've made me feel honored," I sniffed, holding back my tears. When we approached our ride for the night, the driver opened the rear door of the limousine for us. Brazen held my hand, helping me in the limo and sitting beside me. His smile was a mile wide when he stared across at me. He grabbed hold of my hand and gripped it tight.

"I hope I'm giving you the best night of your life, my gorgeous girl. I hope everything I have planned goes smoothly." Deep inside, I was a quivering mess at the night ahead and wondered if she would accept my proposal. It took us about half an hour to arrive at the Italian restaurant I had booked. Our driver had to double park to let us out because most of the car spots were full, and there was no room for his limousine to park.

We got out after our driver opened the door. He told me to ring him when we were finished, and he'd pick us up. He had a spot downtown where he could park while waiting for us to finish. I nodded and told him I would. I grabbed Christa's hand, leading her across the sidewalk to the Little Italy restaurant. I approached the front clerk and said we had a restaurant under Martinez. She looked at her screen and checked us off. She grabbed some menus off the countertop, and we followed her to our quiet table near the middle window seat. I pulled out Christa's chair for her to sit down and sat across from her.

"This looks like a nice little intimate restaurant, Babe. Have you been before? I asked him.

"Nope, first time I've been here. But a good acquaintance has and thoroughly recommended it for a romantic evening. He said it was the perfect spot for a romantic dinner for two. It appears he wasn't wrong. What would you like to drink, my love? A bottle of wine or something else?"

"A bottle of wine sounds good. I'll let you pick something, okay? I love a nice wine but am no connoisseur, so I wouldn't know what to pick."

"Sure thing, like you think I'm a wine expert," I laughed while I perused the wine menu. I decided to pick a nice, expensive bottle of champagne to celebrate the occasion.

The next thing I knew, our server, who introduced herself as Monique, appeared at our table.

"Are you ready to order, Sir or do you need more time?"

"Ummm, a little more time, please. However, we will have a bottle of the Domaine de La Pousse D'or Bonnes Mares Grand Cru. Thank you, Monique."

"Thank you, Sir. I will organize your wine bottle with the waiter, who will bring it to your table. I will be back shortly to take your food order when you are ready to order," she smiled and left.

"Do you see anything that you like on the menu, Baby? Will we have a starter or just a main meal and dessert?

"Hmmm, an entrée to share and a main course. I'll see if I can fit dessert in after that," I grinned.

How does the Gnocchi Modenese for a starter sound to you?"

"Mmmm, that sounds delicious, babe. We'll start with that. I think I will have the Agnello, that sounds delicious for my main. What about you, handsome? What are you going to have for your main course?"

"I'm not sure it all sounds so good. Your one sounds good, but I might try the Cervo and some of yours." I grinned cheekily at Christa."

I shook my head at the cheek of this man of mine. "Whatever Babe" I commented. "You better share some of yours with me, too."

Our wine waiter arrived, showing me the bottle for my approval that he had the correct bottle I had ordered. I nodded in the affirmative. He poured some into my wine glass for me to taste. I took a tentative sip, blowing my taste buds away with a burst of flavor. "Delicious, thank you." I nodded, and he filled my glass. He then turned and filled Christa's. I raised my glass and toasted her, "Happy Birthday, Gorgeous and to a wonderful year ahead." She clinked my glass, and we both took a sip.

"Wow, Brazen this is delicious. You sure know your wines."

"Maybe one of many talents, Gorgeous" I winked. At that moment, Monique arrived and took our food order. We sat there chatting while waiting for our starter to arrive. My nervousness increased while I stared into her eyes, wondering how she would take my proposal.

Monique arrived back, bursting our romantic bubble with our starter. It was delicious, melting in the mouth and overwhelming the taste buds with flavor. Our main meals were just as delicious when delivered to our table by the lovely Monique. With the ever-increasing lump in my throat, I found it hard to swallow my food now. Since the moment to propose was nearly here. When we had finished our main course, I waited until Monique cleared our plates away, asking us if we would like dessert. I told her, "I'm not sure, but bring us the menu, and we will have a look. Thank you."

I cleared my throat, stood up, and walked over toward Christa...

"Brazen, what are you doing? Oh god, you're not. Brazen, you're starting to scare me now," my tummy doing flip flops and butterflies going wild in my stomach. My heart was pounding in my chest. At the same time, the background noise drowned out the noise here in our own little bubble. Everyone in the restaurant must have realized what was about to happen and went silent, adding to the tense atmosphere.

I went down on my left knee and rested my right arm on my right knee. I pulled the box out of my left pocket and held it, ready to show her the ring at the right moment. I looked up into her eyes. "Christa, my love. I know we met under auspicious circumstances, unlike how most other people meet in their lives. But I felt you as soon as I saw you. I knew then that you were my soulmate. I'm sure we knew each other in a past life, and we were meant to find each other and be together again in this life. I love you, baby. Please be mine." I smiled when she clapped her hands to her mouth, and I could see the tears pricking at her eyes. "You melted the ice and broke the chains around my heart. I thought I would never feel for any woman what I feel for you. You have had to put up with me and the darkness around me. You helped me see into the light with your love. I would be honored if you would do the honor of becoming my wife and let us be together for the rest of our lives." I lifted the lid on the ring box and waited for her response.

"Oh, my god Brazen, that is beautiful. Yes, of course, I will marry you. No doubt about that." I realized then the whole restaurant must have been watching us, and the entire place broke into clapping, wolf whistles, and cheers, making me go bright red while I could feel my blushing cheeks burning. Brazen took my hand and placed the most beautiful ring I had ever seen on my finger. It was platinum gold and a brilliant-cut single diamond with smaller diamonds circling the band. "Oh, Brazen words fail me; it's beautiful, and I will treasure this beautiful ring; you are mine forever." I reached down, encircling him in my arms, where he knelt on the floor, smothering his face in butterfly kisses.

"Thank you, Baby, you have made my day, and you are my whole world," I whispered to her. I then stood up and kissed her deeply, leaving her breathless. I went to my chair and pulled it over, setting it down next to her chair. I grabbed her hand, holding it tight between mine and never wanting to let go. I was glad she had agreed to be mine, and I would never allow her to regret her decision to be with me. Monique came back enquiring if we would like desserts after congratulating us both. I told her we would pass on desserts and have the bill thank you. I reached over and picked up my wine glass. I picked Christa's glass up, handing it to her. I clinked her glass. "Congratulations to us, Baby and thank you for accepting my proposal."

"Never any doubt, Handsome. I love you so much more than anyone I ever have before. I can't believe how lucky I was to find you. My hero was there to rescue me from that hellhole I was being held in and changed my life forever."

I grinned at her. "I hope I've made your day a happy one, baby. I'll text our driver to come and pick us up."

"More than you will ever know, Brazen" staring at the ring on my finger, not believing what had just happened. It was the best day of my life, and he had spoilt me with all my birthday gifts, now topping it off with a beautiful engagement ring."

"Okay," pulling her up with her hand in mine. "Let's go settle the bill and wait for our driver. He will be here in five minutes." I paid at the front desk, and we stood on the sidewalk waiting for our limo. He arrived two minutes later. I waited for him to get out and open the door for us. I helped Christa in the limo first. Before I joined her inside, I whispered to the driver. "Take the long way home and make sure it's a slow ride home," I winked at him.

"Gotcha," he grinned, shutting the door behind me when I got in the limo.

Let's say our driver made true to his promise. While I made good on mine, ravishing Christa in the back of the limo while we took the long, slow way home. It was a marvelous end to our beautiful, romantic evening. I planned on showing her even more when we got home. I can tell you that night, not much sleep was had by us.

Chapter Seventeen – Brazen & Christa

"Mmmm," I stretched out, still in a happy afterglow from our marvelous sexy night together. Brazen must have let me sleep in today. It appeared to be late afternoon, with the bright sun blazing through our bedroom window. I was glad he had allowed me to sleep in due to me aching all over but in the most delicious way. He had kept me awake most of the night. I don't know where he gets his stamina from. I put my arm out to pat the bed to see if my handsome fiancée was still in bed. But alas, no, he wasn't. Disappointed, I sighed and raised my left hand to look at my new engagement ring again. It sent rainbow colors dazzling throughout the bedroom, with the sun catching the cut diamond. I was so lucky. I had a man who loved me and spoilt me very much. I should get up, shower, and search for my fiancée. God, I loved that he was now my fiancée. I loved him so much. My heart burst with pride at my remarkable man. I found him down in the kitchen eating lunch. "Good afternoon, my fiancée. Boy, I love saying it, too." I grinned while glancing at my beautiful ring.

I smiled. She made me so happy, "Afternoon, my gorgeous fiancée. How are you doing this afternoon? I missed you. I let you sleep since I kept you awake most of the night deep in you."

"Mmmm, me too, handsome. I was exhausted by the time you had finished. I felt like a wobbly jelly. I reached for you when I woke up to continue some more of last night. But you were gone..."

I glanced at my watch, grinning, "There is still time..."

"Nah, the moment has passed. I'm hungry now." I reached out, pinching half of his sandwich off the plate.

"Hey, that's mine, woman. Taking liberties now that you're my fiancée, huh!"

"Yes," I grinned. "I'll go make another couple of sandwiches since you're being a meanie and not sharing." I grabbed a plate and made some more bacon sandwiches, putting them on my plate when done, then went over and sat next to Brazen.

"So, baby when would you like to get married?"

I leaned my head on my hand and looked at him. "I have no idea handsome. I hadn't managed to think that far ahead. What about you? Do you have any ideas in mind for a date?"

"Me," pointing to my heart. "Hell, I would marry you tomorrow, baby. But you might want to plan a big wedding, and I have no idea how long that would take. Whenever you want to do is fine with me."

Hmmm I was thinking to myself. I don't even remember if I ever thought about having a big wedding before. I know I have my dad, but we're no longer close. I never bothered contacting him when Brazen rescued me. I don't know, even if he's still looking for me still or never bothered. Maybe he didn't even know that I had been kidnapped. Perhaps I should contact him. I sighed. Do I even want to be under his thumb once again? I know Brazen would not be his choice for a husband for me. I loved Brazen more than I had loved anyone ever before.

"Penny, for your thoughts, baby. You look deep in thought there, and that big sigh you just made didn't sound good." At the same time, I wondered what was going through her mind. I hope she's not having any doubts about us getting married.

"Sorry," rubbing my hand up and down his thigh. "I was just thinking I had never really thought about a big wedding. I never thought I would find anyone wanting to marry me. Then I thought, should I contact my dad to see if he wanted to get involved? But I soon shut that down. I believe he would disapprove of me marrying you. I would never approve of any choice he made for me for a husband. Especially now that I have found the love of my life. We should make it easy without arguments, elope, and get married in the county courthouse, Handsome."

I wrapped my arms around her, kissing her on the forehead. "Baby, I'd marry you in a heartbeat. But it might take us a couple of days to organize. But let's do it. Then we can go somewhere for a few days for our honeymoon. Or, if you wanted all the bells and whistles, we could elope to Vegas. But I would prefer to do it locally if that's okay with you."

"Yeah! I want to make us legal as soon as possible, handsome."

"Okay, county courthouse it is. Now I guess you will have to go shopping again to find a pretty little dress to get married in again."

"Oh no! Not another shopping trip," slapping my hand on my forehead. "how will I cope?" I groaned.

I threw my head back in laughter. "I'm sure you will cope, baby. Money is no object, so don't worry about the cost. Plus, you will need some shoes too. Don't forget those now."

"Can't you go shopping for me, handsome?" *I wouldn't say I liked shopping and would rather buy things online than go to a store.*

"Thanks, baby, but I'll pass. I hate shopping too. Plus, I would likely buy the wrong size or something you didn't like."

I sat there pondering his statement and decided he was right. He would be a terrible shopper for my dress. "Well, I guess I could ring Sherry to see if she will come shopping with me." I had grown close to Sherry and loved volunteering at her women's shelter. I grabbed my cell off the table, bringing up Sherry's name in my contacts, and rang her. "Hi Babe, it's me. I have some good news and bad news for you."

"Okay, that sounds a bit ominous, Girlie. Uh! Much as I hate to say, it hit me with the bad news first."

"Oh, okay, you're going to go there first, huh! Okay, you have drawn the short straw to come dress shopping with me."

"Gee, that's the bad news. I'm too scared to ask what the good news is then," I giggled. "You're not pregnant, are you?"

"Damnit it, you guessed," I giggled. "Nope it's not that. But first, I must ask, are you sitting down?"

"Oh, this is the good news, not the bad news. No, but give me a minute," while I walked across the room to sit at the dining table. I pulled a chair out and sat down. "Okay, girlie I'm sitting down now for you. Hit me with it."

"Okay, Brazen asked me to marry him last night, and I said yes." I had to pull my cell away from my ear with the squealing Sherry was making on the other end deafening me."

"Omg," I squealed in excitement and happiness. "Oh my god, I'm so happy for you both. It couldn't happen to two nicer people that I know. I never thought I would see the day Brazen would ever ask someone to marry him. He sure deserves to have found such happiness in his life with you. Likewise, as do you with Brazen with all you've been through. I'm so glad you both found each other. Oh god, I'm so excited for you both. I hope I manage to score an invite to the wedding bash."

"Well, no invite since we've decided to elope. However, since we need two witnesses, I want you to come away with us and be my witness."

"Omg," throwing my arm across my chest and feeling tears pricking my eyes. I couldn't believe someone felt that much of me to ask them to be there to help them at their wedding. "I've never been to a wedding in my life. I would be honored to be your witness, my friend," I sobbed.

"Hey, no tears, Sher. I love you, and you're my only best friend. Today we will be going shopping for a dress for you and me. We will cover all your expenses to come with us to wherever Brazen decides to surprise me with. I'm so sorry. I didn't mean to make you cry, my sweet friend."

"Believe me, they're tears of happiness, and I'd love to come dress shopping with you. When are we going today or tomorrow?"

"Today, if you're free or the notice is too short, we can make it tomorrow or another day this week."

"No today is good. I can be free at about 10 a.m. I have a few things to tidy up. It's a bit quiet here today. I have some volunteers I can leave to run things while we're out shopping."

"Good, it's a date then. I'll pick you up at ten Sher."

"Great. I'll see you then."

Chapter Eighteen - Christa

I was so excited to be meeting with Sherry to go dress shopping. It made getting married even more exciting now. This was happening. I got the keys to the new convertible Brazen had brought for me and kept quiet about it since he wanted to surprise me. That man of mine, I don't know how I put up with spoiling me all the time. I pulled out of the garage and drove to Sherry's house. She was waiting out the front, too looking as excited as I was to be going shopping. When I pulled up next to her at the curb, she got in excitedly, saying to me.

"Oooh, this is new. I haven't seen Brazen out in this car before."

"I know birthday come engagement gift he got for me. Since you know no way, I am riding a bike and not the van either, I was informed," I explained to Sherry while rolling my eyes. "Do you know of any wedding dress shops in the area, Sherry? You've been here your whole life, and I'm new to the area."

"Yes, not here, though it's over in Charleville. Which is the next village over; they have a lovely wedding attire shop that's quite popular. Most people from town here go there to get all their wedding outfits."

"Well, Charleville, it is then. How long will it take us to get there in the car?"

"Hmmm, maybe about an hour, depending on traffic."

"Okay, how about halfway there, we find a coffee shop to have a snack and coffee? We need to get our strength up for all this shopping we must do, huh?" I giggled.

"Yeah, that sounds like a good plan." I smiled back at Christa. "I'm so happy for you both, honey. It couldn't happen to a more lovely couple than you two."

"Thanks, Sher," I smiled. "I can't believe how lucky I am either. I was fortunate that my forever man rescued me from a fate worse than death, and here we are now, happy and in love."

"Yeah, such a romantic story you both have, Girlie."

"Okay, this place looks fine. Do you think Sherry for a break?" When we were about thirty minutes into our drive.

"Uh-huh! This is fine and looks popular. I hope we find a table in there, Honey."

We will or annoy someone who's by themselves to allow us to sit at their table," I smirked.

"Do that often, do you?" I giggled.

"Oh, hell yeah. It's a good way to meet people by yourself too. I used to do that in my past life," I sighed.

"Do you want to talk about it, Babe?"

"No," I was adamant about that. "Sorry, I didn't mean to be a bit short towards you, Sher. I want to leave the past in the past. Maybe I'm doing the wrong thing by cutting my father totally out of my life. But I feel he did the same to me when I was all he had left after my mother and brother died. Anyway, enough Debbie downer, let's go inside and have something to eat." I unclicked my belt and exited the car, with Sherry following close behind. I approached the server near the door, asking if there were any spare tables. She looked around and pointed to one near the back. I guess that will have to do. I thought it was busy in here after all. We sat down at the table and looked at the menus. "What are you going to have, Sherry? Have anything you like or as much as you want Brazen's paying, of course." I grinned. "I think I might have the peach cobbler with cream and a coffee with cream," I advised our server, Debbie, when she came to take our order.

"Hmmm... I might have the apple pie and ice cream with a black coffee. Thank you, Debbie" after giving her my order. When she left to organize our order, I asked Christa "do you have any ideas on what you envision your wedding dress to look like?"

"No not as such! I'm no virgin, so I won't wear white. I know it doesn't matter, but... Ummm, I don't like cream either," I sighed. "

I think I might go for something in red or black. I want something different instead of the norm."

"I like that idea. I like people who dare to be different and wear bold colors like red or black."

"Thanks, me too. Tell me, Sherry, have you got a man hidden somewhere we don't know about?" I wanted to put her on the spot while out of her comfort zone to see if she would let slip that she did.

"Hell, no, Honey. I don't have time for a man. I am too busy running my woman's refuge to find time for a man. Less trouble, too when you don't have one in your life, let me tell you."

"That's sad. You deserve to have a nice man who worships you." At that moment, Debbie returned with our coffee, pie, and bill. "Mmmmm, they smell delicious thanks, Debbie" I smiled. We sat in a comfortable silence, eating our desserts and sipping our coffee. When we had finished, I pulled some cash out and left enough for Debbie, giving her a hefty tip for her lovely service. "Let's hit the road now and get to that bridal shop, Sher. I must admit I'm starting to get nervous now. I feel sick." We left the restaurant and walked back to my car.

"It's not too late to change your mind now, Honey."

"I know," I giggled. "I love him so much. I can't not." I started the car and drove back on the highway on our way to Charleville to the wedding shop. We had an excellent run-through with hardly any traffic along the way. Sherry gave me directions to the shop. I parked out the front of the shop since it was on the main street. We got out and entered the quaint little shop. I was stunned at the wide range of everything wedding they had in store. It was deceiving the size of the shop from the street. It looked bigger inside than it did from the front.

I took a glance around, deciding where to start. I gasped and grabbed hold of Sherry's hand. I pulled her along with me to the rear of the store.

"Is everything okay, Christa?" I wondered why she had gasped and dragged me to the rear of the store. What had she seen?

"I've found it, Sherry." I practically dragged her over to the dress I had just noticed. I know I said I didn't want white, but technically, it's not and looks stunning." We stood in front of the dress, and I stared with my mouth open. It was a sleeveless white dress with a deep V front and back. But the whole dress was overlaid with red leaves, making it look amazing. "I need this one, Sherry. I love it".

"Yes, even I love it too. It's going to suit you, Christa. Even I can envision you in this beautiful dress. You are going to rock that dress."

"Can I help you ladies? I'm Jean, the store owner. Sorry for the delay, ladies. I was caught up on a phone call. Are you interested in this little number?"

"Yes," I breathed out. "I love it, Jean, and I want it. Do you think it will fit me? I need it in a hurry. My fiancée and I only recently decided to elope, and I need a dress urgently."

"Yes, I think it should fit you fine, dear. Sorry, I missed your name honey."

"Sorry, I'm Christa, and this is my friend and maid of honor to be Sherry."

"I'm pleased to meet you ladies. If we need to make any adjustments, there's plenty of room to take it out if we need to. I always try to be generous with the seams with my ready-made dresses. I make everything in-store in the dress line anyway. I can make to order, but that option is out since you're in a hurry for your dress. If you would like to go in the changing room, Christa and I will be there shortly with the dress for you."

"Thanks," I gushed excitedly. I didn't even know what I wanted until I saw it. I went into the dressing room and took my jeans and top off, ready to try on the dress. I heard a knock on the door.

"It's only me, Christa. Are you decent for me to come in with the dress?"

"Yes, I've dressed down to my underwear, but I'm decent."

Jean entered with the dress, hanging it up on the hook on the wall and unzipping the zipper on the back. I helped Christa with the dress, then zipped it back up. "You look stunning, Christa. Now I think the gown fits you perfectly. I'll go and grab my pins. We will need to shorten it slightly. Do you have any shoes to wear so I can shorten it to the correct length?"

"Ummm, no I don't. Do you have any in-store Jean that would go with the dress?"

"Yes, I think I have a white lacy pair that will go with this dress. What size shoe do you take?"

"Size nine, thanks Jean."

I went to the rear storeroom and found a size nine in the shoe I had in mind. On the way past, I grabbed my pins off the back desk. I knocked on the door "it's only me again, Christa," I opened the door and entered the dressing room. I lifted the lid on the shoes I had picked out, showing Christa, "are you happy to try these shoes I picked for you?"

"Oh my gosh, yes. They're beautiful." I picked them out of the box and put them on, and they fit perfectly.

Meanwhile, I got down on the floor with my pot of pins and began pinning her dress up for shortening to the correct length with the right shoes on. Once that was done, I stood up again. "Would you like to go and show your friend Sherry how you look now that we're all done? I'm sure you want her approval before you take everything off?"

"Yes, thanks Jean." I hitched the dress up, opened the door, and called Sherry, who was busy looking at dresses. "Hey, Sherry, what do you think?"

"Omg, Christa, you look stunning in that dress. Brazen isn't going to know what hit him when he sees you in that dress, honey." Now we need to find something for me to wear now. I'm spoilt for choice here; I don't know what to pick. I'm going to need your help."

"Just give me a minute then. I'll take this dress off and put my other clothes back on, then I'll join you." I entered the dressing room and took everything off, ready for Jean. Once she had left the changing room, I put my clothes back on and went to help Sherry with her choice of dress. We found one Sherry was happy with after searching a few dress racks. It was a red that matched the leaves on my dress. It was off the shoulder on the left side, and on the right side, it was over the shoulder with one sleeve down to the elbow. The bodice was laced with a leaf pattern, and across the bodice, under the lace and the skirt, which was mid-length, were made of satin silk. Sherry went and tried it on. The dress fit perfectly. Jean didn't need to make any changes to Sherry's dress. We also picked out a pair of red silky shoes to go with Sherry's dress.

After ringing up my purchases and paying for them, Jean advised me that she would prioritize my dress and start on it tomorrow and asked if I could come back Thursday afternoon to try on for size, making sure to bring the shoes with me, too. I promised her I would. I told her I might as well leave the shoes here. Then, I didn't need to worry about forgetting them on Thursday. She laughed and agreed with me.

Sherry and I left the store with Sherry's dress and shoes since hers didn't need any altering. We got back in my car and began the journey back home. Fortunately for us, it was a smooth ride home. I dropped Sherry off at the shelter and drove home to my man.

Chapter Nineteen – Brazen

I groaned when my phone pinged with a message when I was nearly asleep. I half rolled over to grab my phone off the nightstand. Shit, a message from Mo. It had better be urgent to interrupt me at this time of night.

Mo: Problem. We need to head out to the warehouse.

Me: Important enough for me to head out to? I knew I must be present since I'm the club president. But I just had to yank his chain while I was at it.

Mo: You need to ask?

Me: No, but I had to yank your chain.

Mo: Hurry up, get your dick out of your woman, and get downstairs NOW.

Me: Oooh, shouty caps. You're mad. I was asleep. Coming now.

MO: Yeah, sure. Remember that the walls are not soundproof around here.

Me: Yeah! Yeah! I'm coming down now.

I reluctantly extracted myself from her arms wrapped around my chest. "Sorry, baby, I need to go out. Urgent business," I whispered in her ear. She groaned at me but didn't stir from her sleep. I got up and sat on the edge of the bed, rubbing my eyes, then stood up. I retrieved my jeans off the floor and pulled them on. I grabbed a clean shirt and a pair of socks from the walk-in robe. I put them on and walked out of the bedroom, quietly shutting the door behind me.

I jogged down the stairs and met Mo in the main room. "What's going on, Mo?" I inquired.

"There's been a break-in at the warehouse, and the few men on patrol were injured. I'm sure whoever it was, they were sending a message. Since it appears that they didn't bother to kill our men, we might have to up security there until we discover who it was and what they want."

"Yeah. I have no idea currently who has a grudge against us. I haven't heard any whispers of anyone having a problem with us. Well, not yet. We better head out there and take more men with us. You round them up, and I'll meet you out the front. I'll go out and have a quick smoke first."

"Yep, they're ready. Like you, they're all grabbing a smoke out the back."

"Okay, I better be quick then," I grinned.

Before long, we were all assembled out the front, hopped on our bikes, and ready to go to the warehouse to see what was happening there. The place was messy when we arrived at our warehouse, with some boxes thrown around. Out in the front carpark, it appeared it was empty. However, when we entered the warehouse, we discovered a few of our men were lying injured on the floor. Doc was already here tending to their wounds.

"Mo, call one of the guys on the gate to bring the van out here so we can take the injured men home. They don't look like they'll be riding their bikes home. We'll lock their bikes up here in the warehouse. We can return later to take them back in a van to the compound.

Further, to add to my disappointment in being called out here. It seemed the men who had been here and ambushed my men were in and out, then gone. They had long disappeared since it was a while before anyone here could raise the alarm. Since we could not find them anywhere. It seemed they had broken into the warehouse without setting any alarms off and hid, waiting to ambush my men when they showed up. One of my men, who was now conscious, advised me what had happened. There was no trace of them hiding on the grounds either. Is it a setup? If so, who was behind it? I would have Mo sniff out any intel about what had gone on tonight and see who was behind it. We could check the security cameras, but I'm betting they would be dressed to avoid detection and hide their identity from the cameras. I'd also put some feelers out with some of our allies and warn them in case they became targets. "Hey Mo, I'm heading back home. I'll leave you here to sort the van out when it arrives. I'll see you when you get back. I'll head back and check the security cameras. However, if they're pro, they will hide their identity. But I'll give it a shot."

"Okay, Braze. More like going back to keep the little woman warm, huh?"

"Shut up you! Stop tempting me. Let me know when you return, and we'll meet in my office." I started my bike and went home to the little woman. I was fully intending to keep her warm in our bed. But first, I would check the security footage quickly, though I knew it would be pointless. I was right. They were all dressed in black, wearing hoodies and masks to hide their identity. Once that was done, I retired to bed, waiting for Mo to return.

Chapter Twenty - Brazen

I heard my phone ping with a message at about 4 a.m. I rolled over to see another message from Mo advising me they had arrived back at the compound. I reluctantly eased myself from my haven in Christa's arms, rolling over and getting out of bed. I wandered downstairs to my office. "Mo," I acknowledged him with a chin lift when I saw him waiting in there already. I went and sat in my chair behind the desk. "How's things? More importantly, how are the men who were injured?"

"Nothing too serious and nothing major that they can't cope with. All the men are back in their rooms, tucked up in bed. Doc will return in the morning to check them over. Mainly superficial wounds and a couple of concussions. I think they were wanting to give us a message. We need to find out who was behind the ambush. I'll put the word out and let you know if I hear anything."

"Great! I'll check around in my inner circles to see if any birdies out there are ready to sing. Someone out there knows something. We need to find out who it is. Another thing while I've got you pinned down, too. I was going to ask you to come away with us for a yet-to-be-determined weekend to be a witness at my wedding. Now, much as I want you there at my wedding. I'm not sure it would be a good time to have us both away together."

"What things were you planning for your wedding?" I asked, curious to see what he had in mind.

"Well, we had thought about running away to elope and go away for the weekend. Neither of us wanted a big wedding. It's not us. We want something small, intimate, and private. We need a couple of witnesses. Christa has her one sorted in Sherry." I grinned knowingly at Mo. I threw my head back, laughing when he scowled at me, and if I'm not mistaken, I'm sure I heard a growl in there, too. "I was planning on you being my best man and witness. Then maybe have a big party after we come back to include everyone. What do you think?"

"Don't do that! Why not hold it here? We can get someone in from outside to cater to it. Then only invite a select few you would like to have attend your wedding. That way, it won't be a problem security-wise to get married outside the compound after tonight's events. It would be easier regarding security holding your wedding here at the compound rather than somewhere unknown," I explained to Brazen since I felt we didn't need to make ourselves an easier target for our unknown enemy.

I sat there, steepling my fingers on my chin. "Mmmm... yes, that sounds like a great idea. It's maybe not quite as romantic as we had planned. But like you said after tonight, putting anyone at risk is not a good idea, especially if we plan to marry outside of the community. Well, you've sold me. I'll run it by Christa in the morning to ensure she's okay with it, too." I slammed my hands down on the desk, standing up. "Well, if that's everything for now, I'll head back to bed."

"Pussy whipped," I muttered under my breath at Brazen.

"What was that you said? I hope it wasn't what I think it was," I glared at Mo.

"Nothing, you big pussy. Hurry up and get back to that woman of yours. I will have a shot, then head off to bed myself. Night. I'll see you later when you get up to grace us with your presence."

"Uh-huh! Night, see you tomorrow. Pussy whipped my ass," I uttered, walking past Mo on the way out of my office. I went back up the stairs two at a time to my bedroom, snuck back into bed, wrapped my arms around Christa, and instantly fell asleep. I slept right through to morning. Even my gorgeous girl was awake before me. When I opened one eye, I saw her lying on her pillow, staring me in the face. "Morning Gorgeous." I smiled and kissed her hard on the lips. I rolled over, bringing her with me so she was lying beside me. I smiled and tucked her hair behind her ears. "How was I so lucky to find a gorgeous ray of sunshine to settle down with?"

"It's fate, I'm sure of it. I thank god every day that you found me, baby. I have my life to thank you for. I don't know what would have happened to me in Torres's hellhole basement."

"Yeah, let's not think about that now and put a dampener on things. Mo came up with an idea for our wedding. Instead of eloping, we should hold it here to have a small, private, intimate affair. Where can we feel safe and have the people we want here to witness our nuptials? I don't want to scare you, baby, but we might have an unknown enemy after us here. We don't know who it is, so it might be safer to have it here. I know it may not be what you want. But your safety is critical to me. I hope you'll be okay with the new plans."

I kissed him, saying, "I'll be happy with your plans, Handsome. I'm marrying the man of my dreams and couldn't be happier. So that's a yes from me. We can always have a honeymoon later when things are safe."

I smiled. "I'm lucky, too. I get to marry the woman of my dreams." I smiled up at her and then slapped her on the ass cheeks. "Come on then, Gorgeous, let's get up, and I'll cook you some breakfast. I know it's the afternoon, but breakfast's never too late. How does bacon, eggs, and waffles sound?"

"Perfect." I rolled off him and onto my side of the bed. "I can't believe I even get a man that cooks too. How much more perfect can you be, Handsome?"

"Well, I think I'm good in the sack and know how to keep my woman happy. Sorry if it sounds a bit caveman, but it's true," I winked.

"Mmmmm, I can't argue with my sexy caveman who knows how to hit all the right spots and how to pleasure me. Well, I shall shower and see you in the kitchen while you go down and make me breakfast."

"Well, hurry up then, woman, before I burn breakfast when I get there." I got up, threw on a pair of jeans and a T-shirt, then headed downstairs to cook my favorite woman's breakfast.

Chapter Twenty One – Brazen & Christa

I made myself busy cooking bacon and eggs in the pan. I put the premade waffles in the toaster to heat and toast while the other food cooked in the pan. I heard a noise. "Ah, here she is, my gorgeous girl." I leaned over to kiss her lips when she got closer, wrapping her arms around my waist.

"Mmmm, smells delicious, Handsome. I didn't realize my hunger until I smelt breakfast cooking." My stomach gave me away at that moment by growling.

"Take a seat, Gorgeous. It's ready now. I just gotta put it on our plates." I dished everything up on the plates and took our plates over to the breakfast bar where Christa now sat.

"Mmmm, this is delicious, Brazen. If I knew you were such a great cook, I would have married you sooner," I laughed.

"You're welcome, Gorgeous," I grinned. "I would have too if I knew you would love my cooking. Soon, baby soon. Not long now." We both sat in comfortable silence, eating our breakfast. Once we had finished, Christa went to load the dishwasher with our plates since I had cooked. I didn't mind; I got to watch that delicious curvy ass of hers each time she bent down to load more in there. Fuck if she didn't hurry up, I might take her over that countertop when I felt my cock twitching in my jeans. "Hurry up, Gorgeous. I'll give you a two-minute head start. You get yourself up those stairs and naked in our bed. I now have some morning wood that I need to get rid of. Starting now..."

I squealed and then laughed before I got myself into action and took off running up the stairs. I never had so much fun with a lover, and I loved this. I decided I might be a bit of a brat and leave my panties on. I wonder what he will do to me for not being completely naked in bed. What punishment will he deal out to me? I lay there giggling when I heard him running up the steps two at a time by the sounds. My two minutes must be up. I'm sure I must have had a smile a mile wide when I saw that vision of my handsome, sexy man out of breath leaning against the door frame.

"Well, what do we have here? Gorgeous, I thought I told you to be naked when I arrived." I stalked towards her before stopping and standing at the end of the bed, putting my hands on my hips.

I giggled, telling him, "I wanted to test your limits and see what punishment you might bestow on me." I blushed shyly, now suddenly feeling ashamed for what reason I did not know.

My eyes are full of hunger and lust, ready to get my hands on her and take my fill. "Oh, my sweet baby, what did you do to me" my cock straining against my jeans, almost roaring in anger against his confinement. While waiting with impatience to escape his confines. I got even hornier when I didn't think I could anymore. At the same time, my cheeky wench lay there. She dared me when she stared me in the eye, raising an eyebrow and smirking before dropping her raised knees apart. "Oh, fuuuuccccckkk..." I groaned. She lay there showing me her soaking wet panties. "I might forgive you this once only because I don't know if I have it left to give you any punishment now."

I moaned, "Oh fuck, baby. Look how wet you are for me." I ran my finger along the wet crease through her panties. She was so fucking damn wet that I needed to suck my finger clean. I slipped my finger under her panties, pulling them down slightly. I took a sniff of that sweet pussy I wanted to devour. That sweet, musky scent calling out my name like a siren lured me in. I was helpless to resist. I ripped her panties off, causing her to gasp at the audacity of my bold move.

God, I loved everything I did to him, provoking the wild lust deep within him. He was fantastic with desire; I could see it in his dark eyes. It gave me great pleasure to enjoy what I was doing to him and what he did to me. I loved Brazen's reaction when I spread my legs to show him what he did to me. I was so hungry to feel his cock deep in me and take away the need and want I had for him.

I bent down and ran my tongue up her slippery wet pussy licking up the copious amount of juices she had leaking from her sweet cunt. I licked around her swollen nub and gave it a nip.

I groaned, clamping my legs shut around Brazen's head, trapping him there. When he would only be accessible to concentrate on and service my achy needy throbbing clit. He was doing everything to drive me insane by licking and nipping my fucking needy clit. Fuck, it had been so long since I had been treated like this. Knowing I had found my man, it felt like heaven and very freeing. I was glad he found and rescued me, so I was no longer locked in a basement for that madman's pleasure. I had my own sweet man to pleasure and devour me like I didn't know that I needed until now.

Oh, fuck when she clamped her legs around me, trapping my head. If I die now between her legs... I will die here, a happy man. I began licking and sucking her sweet juices to make her come deep and hard. Before I fucked her with my cock, I needed to make her come first. I needed her to cum and fill my mouth with sweet, delicious juices.

I shoved two fingers into her soaking wet cunt while licking and sucking her clit. She had a copious amount of her juices flowing free for me, quenching my thirst for her. I add another finger and start shoved three fingers in that sopping pussy. I thrust them into her pussy to find that elusive spot to make her cum. I could feel her body start to shake with an impending orgasm. Before I knew it, she came squirting for me and drenching me, squirting over me.

I move up her body kissing her sweet body as I go, and then shove my hard, aching cock deep in her cunt. I can't wait any longer. My greedy cock glides in with ease. She is so wet for me. I taste my fingers so delicious. I shove them in her mouth "suck my fingers clean and taste how delectable you are, my love." While I continue thrusting my cock in and out of her hungry cunt while she grips my rock-hard cock tight, needing a release. I am willing for him to come deep inside her. I give one final thrust deep in her and start filling her full of my cum, shooting out my cock deep within her. God, there's so much cum I am beginning to think he will never stop. I gave one final thrust, and he gave her it all. With the vibrations from her pussy rolling around, she managed to milk my cock dry.

"Mmmm," I moan while sucking his fingers deep in my mouth. I continue moving up and down the bed with his cock thrusting deep in me. God, it feels so good with his hard cock pushing, hitting me in all the right spots. I need to come again. He makes me feel so good. He knows all the moves to do to make me cum again and again. I love my man and don't know what I'd do without him anymore. I grip his cock tight when I start coming again along with him. I can feel the ropes of cum thrusting out deep in me. Who knew fucking someone could be this great. I could feel his cock still throbbing and vibrating in my pussy when he still after cumming, filling my pussy with all his cum.

I pull out of her, groaning, and drop onto the bed beside her. "Come here, baby," I breathlessly pulled her close with my left arm. I gripped her tight against my chest. I never want to let her go ever again. She throws her leg over mine, and I feel her wet cunt dripping on my leg. I take advantage and start rubbing her nub again.

"Enough," I told him. "I can't take anymore," I moaned, complaining to him. "I've had enough. I'm exhausted," I pouted.

"Challenge accepted" I grin and start rubbing her clit faster. "Come on, baby cum for me again. You can do it. I know you can." I tried not to laugh when she rocked against my fingers. "I feel you trying to get more friction on your clit from my fingers. Gorgeous. Come on, you can do it. Fuck baby, you're such a horny little witch for me, aren't you? You can't get enough of me." My fingers started to tire from rubbing her so hard that I began willing her to cum. Thankfully, she came for me again with the next rub of my fingers. "There, I told you, didn't I, baby." I kissed her on the forehead and gripped her tighter, never wanting to let go. Even I had to admit I was exhausted and felt myself slowly drifting off to sleep.

Chapter Twenty Two - Christa

Before I knew it, Thursday had come, and it was time to go and revisit Jean. I needed to try my wedding dress on for size. I went by myself since Sherry already had her outfit. Although the company would have been nice, unfortunately, she was busy at the shelter again. This wedding was making me so nervous. I was feeling sick daily. I would be glad when it was all over. I pulled up out the front of Jean's shop and went into the shop. "Hi Jean," I called out when entering her store.

"Hi Christa. I'll be out in a minute. I must finish up some paperwork here. Grab a coffee and a cookie while you wait if you like."

"Thanks, but I'm good. I'll sit on the sofa while waiting for you. Don't rush; I'm in no hurry."

"Okay, thanks" I called back to Christa. When I finished the invoice I was working on, I emailed it to the client. I grabbed Christa's dress and shoes for her to try on again. "Okay, I'm ready, honey. Let's go to the dressing room now and try your outfit."

I got up from the sofa but must have stood up too quickly; I got a bit of a head spin. I stood there briefly before following Jean to the dressing room. I nearly cried when I entered the room and saw my dress hanging with my shoes below them. "Oh, Jean, it looks even better seeing my dress again. I love it even more." I could feel tears pricking my eyes. *Don't cry, girl don't cry.* I put the shoes on after taking my jeans and shirt off. Jean helped me into my dress, and when I looked in the mirror, I stood there looking in awe. I couldn't believe how beautiful I looked in my wedding dress. "Jean, thank you, it fits perfectly. I love my dress."

"I forgot to ask whether you wanted a full veil or just a half veil when you were here last time. Please forgive me for my omission."

"That's fine. I never gave it a thought, either. It's probably because I'm not one for headgear. I was so excited about finding my dress. I think just something short will be fine." I went through the section and found a short one with a headpiece that I was happy with. It completed my outfit for my big day. I took everything off for Jean to bag up for me. Once, I had dressed in my street clothes. I exited the dressing room and walked up to the counter to collect my goods and pay for my veil. Well, I tried, but Jean insisted on making it complimentary, and there was no changing her mind about it. I thanked her profusely and promised to send her a photo of our big day when we had them. I got in my car and drove to Sherry's house to drop my wedding day outfit off to hide in her apartment at the refuge. Then, there was no temptation for Brazen to go searching to see what my outfit looked like.

When I returned home after giving Sherry a fashion show, she packed everything away for Saturday. I suddenly had a thought. I hope Brazen had organized everything for Saturday because I sure hadn't. I went in search of him, but he was nowhere to be found. I went up to bed to lie down due to the fact I was feeling a bit tired. Goodness knows why I felt drained of late. Maybe it was all the excitement of my birthday and forthcoming wedding. "Mmmm," when I felt myself getting butterfly kisses on my face, "hi handsome, where did you come from?"

"I just got home and came here when I couldn't find you? Are you okay? It's not like you to be sleeping in the middle of the day. Well, not unless we've spent most of the night fucking. But as far as I recall, we slept most of the night."

I opened my eyes, staring into his. "I think all the excitement of my birthday and our wedding coming up," I yawned.

"My goodness honey, it sounds like you still need more sleep. I hope you're not coming down with anything. I shall leave you in peace. I'll be back if you're not awake by dinner time, " planting a kiss on her lips and brushing the back of my hand across her forehead.

"I would get up, but I'm too comfy here and need more sleep. I must be getting old," I laughed. I watched him walk out of our bedroom and close my eyes again. I woke later at 4 p.m. I got up and searched for Brazen and found him in his office. "Hey handsome," I said, sitting on his lap when he pushed his chair back from his desk. "Someone is happy to see me," when I felt his rock-hard cock poking in my backside.

"Hey, he's always happy to see you, my gorgeous girl, along with me. What can I do you for?"

"I was wondering if you had organized everything for our wedding on Saturday because I know I've done nothing to help."

"Of course, I have my gorgeous girl. You don't have to worry about a thing. Mo and I have done everything. Anything I felt might need the female touch; I got Valeria to do for me."

I kissed him on the tip of the nose. "Thank you handsome. I can't wait to be your wife. I'm sorry I didn't do anything to help."

"Don't worry about it. You did the most important part of organizing Sherry's and your dresses for the big day. Not much longer now. Are you still planning to stay the night with Sherry on Friday? Then I'm not tempted to look for you and your dress until the right moment."

"Yep. We might have a few drinkies, though not too many. Not that I plan on getting ripped when I'm getting married the next day, I promise."

"I know you will behave gorgeous. Now, do you want to get down on your knees and get rid of this hard-on I'm sporting before dinner? I don't think I will ever be able to get up if I don't get rid of it."

"Hmmmm yessss please," I winked. I slowly slid off his lap, smiling when I heard him groan. I got down on my knees between his legs, undid his belt, and slowly slid his zipper down. Oh, going commando today, baby, I see."

I groaned. "only for you, baby."

I grabbed hold of his cock and slowly licked my tongue around the lip on the tip of his cock. I smiled when some precum leaked out, which

I licked up and continued licking his tip. "Stand up a minute, Baby, so I can pull your jeans down and get at those swollen blue balls, too."

I stood obliging and helped by pulling my jeans down to my knees. I slid forward on the chair, giving her more accessible access to those balls she was desperate to get to.

I grabbed hold of the top of his cock, stroking him while I sucked his balls in my mouth, sucking them deep in my mouth, looking up and staring him in the eyes. They were black with lust. I smiled around his balls with the groans coming from above. I guess he was enjoying what I was doing to him. I stroked his cock up and down with my hand, which pulled his balls out of my mouth on the upward stroke then I sucked them back deep in my mouth. I poked my tongue, stroking the line under his balls while continuing to stroke him up and down while sucking on his balls.

"Fuck baby, where did you learn that? It feels so amazing," I moaned. "Fuck I'm going to come baby," when I felt my balls draw up, preparing to cum.

I kept my sucking action on his balls while tugging his hard cock up and down when I felt him still before pumping his cum all through my hair with his delicious cum. "I hope I did good, baby" when I released his softening cock. I better go have a shower now and wash my hair before dinner."

"I'll come join you and wash your back."

"I don't think so, or we will never make it to dinner with you and your sex drive. I don't know about you, but I'm starving hungry."

Chapter Twenty Three - Christa

Before long, it was Friday, and I packed an overnight bag to spend the night at Christa's place for my last night of freedom. Mo drove me over to Sherry's house. He repeatedly assured me he had everything under control. Everything, including Brazen, would be ready for tomorrow. I promised I wouldn't worry. Although I wish I could eliminate this nauseous feeling. Maybe after we were married, with all the stress and worry out of the way, it would all disappear. Mo pulled up to the front door of Sherry's house, and I got out and walked up the front steps, ringing the doorbell. Sherry must have been busy since she hadn't come out to greet me already. I smiled, ready to welcome Sherry, when the door eventually opened. I tried not to show my disappointment when it was someone else.

"Hi honey, you must be Christa. My name's Ellen, and Sherry sends her apologies. She's tied up with a new lady who was in an emergency and had to take her to the hospital. She should hopefully be back soon. I'll show you to her room to store your things."

"Sorry, I didn't mean to look so disappointed when you opened the door."

"That's fine, honey. I know you were probably expecting Sherry. Follow me up the stairs, and I'll show you to Sherry's room."

I followed her up to Sherry's room on the first floor. When she unlocked the door. I was amazed it was huge. She had a giant king bed in the middle of the room with stunning backyard views. I saw Sherry had set up a single bed for me in the corner and I dumped my bag on top.

"Would you like a coffee and some cookies, honey?"

"Sure, that would be lovely. I'll freshen up in the bathroom and see you there, Ellen." I went and ran the cold tap, splashed some on my face, and dried my face. I went downstairs in search of the kitchen to have my coffee. I found Ellen in the kitchen. "Hi Ellen.'

"Hi honey. I forgot to ask how you have your coffee."

"White with one sugar, thank you. Do you need a hand with anything? I feel bad getting waited on like this."

"That's fine. I don't mind, which means I have a break too." I put the two coffees on the table and went and grabbed the cookie jar off the countertop, placing it between us on the table. "Help yourself to as many cookies as you would like. No shame around here," she smiled.

"Thank you," taking a sip of coffee. "Why does coffee always taste better when you don't make it yourself?" I giggled.

"I know. My sentiments exactly."

We both sat there in a comfortable silence, each lost in their thoughts. I was worrying about how tomorrow would go. Would everything go fine, and hoping nothing would go wrong? I heard the front door open and Sherry calling, "It's only me."

"In the kitchen with Christa," Ellen called out.

"Okay, I'll be there in a minute. I'll drop my bag in my office." I countered back.

"I'll make you a fresh coffee' Ellen yelled back.

"Thanks Honey." I unlocked the bottom drawer in my desk, put my bag in, and relocked the drawer before heading out to the kitchen to join Christa and Ellen. I hugged Christa when she stood up as I entered the kitchen. "Hi Honey, I'm so pleased to see you. Sorry, I wasn't here when you arrived. I had to take an emergency to the hospital, and they're keeping her for a couple of nights. Are you getting nervous about tomorrow?"

"I was wondering when you would finally come up for air," I laughed. "That's fine. These things happen. Yes, I am so nervous. I've been feeling sick all week.

"Damn that's no good. We'll have to try to remedy that later tonight to give you a bit of extra courage for tomorrow. Though you have nothing to worry about, you're marrying that gorgeous man who is very protective of you."

'I know! I'm so lucky, like I can't believe it. If someone had said to me a year ago that I would be marrying the man of my dreams this year, I would have laughed in their face. Now, thanks to a twist of fate. Look where I am now. Sometimes, I even pinch myself to make sure that I'm not dreaming."

"I believe we're having someone over at 10 a.m. tomorrow to do our hair and makeup. Your man has thought of everything to even book that for us. He won't know what hit him when he sees you walking down that aisle tomorrow."

"Thanks" I responded. "I hope so," bouncing my feet up and down on the floor under the table, squealing excitedly. "I assumed the single bed in your room was mine, so I dumped my bag on it."

"Yes, it sure it is, and all good. You know that you can always make yourself at home here."

"Do you mind if I go have a nap Sher? I'm feeling a bit tired.

"Sure. You're not coming down with something, are you? Feeling tired and nauseous. Oh shit!"

"What?" I queried, suddenly worried...

"You wouldn't happen to be pregnant at all, would you?"

"What?" I exclaimed. "No. No way I could be pregnant. Oh shit, maybe. I haven't been taking the pill since Torres kidnapped me. I just thought. Fuck. Fuck. Fuck" squeezing my fingers against my forehead. No not now.

"Give me a moment. I have some pregnancy tests in the first aid room. Then, we can rule it in or out either way. Give me a moment," getting up from my seat and going to the first aid room. I unlocked the door and grabbed a test from one of the supply drawers. I returned to the kitchen with it held tightly in my hand. I passed it over to Christa. "Here you are. Do you want us to go do it now?"

"Yes, please." I groaned.

"Come on then, let's go up to my room." I turned, taking the lead, going up to my room on the first floor.

"God, what am I going to do if I am?" I moaned. I was apprehensive about what Brazen would think. Would he be happy or mad? Would he believe that I had trapped him by getting pregnant? No, he would marry me before I found out about this.

"Calm down, Christa. I can hear your mind working overtime from here, Honey. It won't matter to Brazen if you are. I happen to know Brazen will be the happiest man alive, married to a beautiful, sassy woman and a baby on the way."

"I hope you're right." It was all still weighing heavy on my mind. I went into the bathroom in Sherry's room, taking the pregnancy test with me. I read the instructions, peed on the stick, and then set the timer on my phone. I closed the lid and waited for the timer to go off. My heart pounded a mile a minute while I waited, too scared about the result. When the alarm went off, I was too afraid to look now.

"Everything okay in there," Sherry asked, tapping on the door.

"Yeah! I'm just too scared to look now."

"Do you want to unlock the door and let me in? Then I can come in and look for you."

"Yeah," I got up from the seat and unlocked the door for Sherry.

I rushed into the bathroom when Christa unlocked the door. Christa might be afraid of what the result might be. But I wasn't. I was desperate to know. I wanted it to be positive for the two of them. I grabbed the stick off the countertop to see what the result was. I gasped, closing my eyes, and held it to my chest. I was happy for my two friends, and the result was positive.

"W-w-what is it? I stammered. "Is it good or bad Sher?"

"Well, it depends on what way you want to go. If it were me, I would be pleased. Congratulations Honey, it's positive." I grabbed her tight in a hug.

"Oh god! I'm trying to take it all in. A wedding. N-n-n-now, a baby." I was happy but scared all at once. "D-d-do you think Brazen will be happy, Sher? Or will he be mad at me because I got pregnant?"

I grabbed Christa by the shoulders. "Look at me, Honey. He will be the happiest man on earth when he learns the news. Please don't blame yourself Honey. It takes two to tango, and he has as much responsibility as you to use birth control if he doesn't want the result of a baby. Please stop blaming yourself and be happy, okay."

"Yeah, thank you, I think. It's just a lot to take in with the wedding, and now we'll have a baby." I grinned, happy at the prospect we were having a baby. "Shall I ring him and tell him now?"

"No. We wait until tomorrow. Then we or you find the perfect moment to tell him. You will know when that moment comes. I promise you." I smiled. I was happy for Christa and Brazen. They deserved all this happiness. "Now, didn't you mention needing a nap? How about you settle down and rest up? I'll pop up and tell you when it's time for dinner if you're asleep."

"Thanks, Sher. I guess that explains everything with the nausea and the tiredness."

"Yep! I'll see you soon, honey," I shut the door behind me, leaving Christa in peace.

Chapter Twenty Four - Christa

I woke refreshed and headed downstairs to find Sherry. I was excited, my heart exploding with happiness. Now I was having a baby and getting married. I found Sherry in her office. Before entering, I knocked on the door in case she was too busy to talk.

"Come in, Honey. Are you feeling better about everything now?" while peering over the top of my glasses perched on the end of my nose.

"Yeah," I gushed excitedly. "I think ecstatic might be the right word. Now I've had time to get used to the news. I can't wait to share the good news with Brazen tomorrow..."

"Yeah, he will be over the moon with the news. Well, I guess drinking is out of the question now. I better get some sodas to drink instead now."

"Yeah, sorry about that. Please feel free to drink alcohol if you wish. You don't have to abstain for my benefit."

"I know, but I will. I don't want to be a drunk maid of honor and embarrass you honey. Not that I planned on doing that anyway. I'll keep you company drinking sodas, though."

"Okay, if you're sure, Sher." I still felt guilty about spoiling her night with me being pregnant. At the same time, Sherry caught up on some work. I left to sit in the loungeroom and read my latest romance book on my tablet to take my mind off things. When Sherry had finished, she came past me in the loungeroom, telling me...

"I'll be back soon." I disappeared upstairs to my room, went to the closet, and pulled a box of goodies out that I had stored there. I pulled out some balloons with "bride to be" on them, using my balloon pump to inflate. I pulled out a white veil with 'bride to be" written on it, which I lay out on the bed. I know we were staying home, but that didn't mean we couldn't have fun and dress up. I pulled out my red one with "maid of honor" on it and put it on my head. I got out the packet of peen straws for us to sip our drinks. I snuck downstairs and brought up nibblies for us to snack on: candy, chocolate, and a couple of soda bottles. I placed a variety for us to enjoy on my nightstand. There, that looks good. I picked up Christa's veil and took it downstairs to pop on her head before taking her back upstairs.

I went to the loungeroom to collect her. "Come on, Honey, time to have some fun," while holding up the veil I had ready for her to wear.

"Omg, you didn't," I laughed, turning red with embarrassment when I looked up from my book to see what Sherry held in her hand.

"Yes, I did. Now get up so I can place it on your head." Once she stood up, I placed the clip on her head and adjusted the veil. "Right, that looks good. Now it's time for a couple of selfies." I pulled my cell phone out of my pocket and snapped pictures. "I'll send the pics to you later, then you have a copy for yourself. Shall I send one to Brazen to show him what we're up to?"

"Yeah, why not?" I giggled. "Add on there; we're off to the male strip club. I hope he gets jealous when he reads that."

"Oooh, yes, I love that idea."

I sent the message to Brazen with the photo of us both and Christa's suggested message.

(B) **Have a great night Girls and behave**

(S) **I dunno it is her hen night. One last fling**

I had to stir the pot while Christa and I giggled over our text chat.

(B) **Grrrrr... do I have to come there and follow you around all night?**

(S) **No we can look after ourselves**

(B) **Right that's it! Mo and I are getting on our bikes to come protect and escort you ladies to ensure you keep safe.**

(S) **Keep your hair on, Samson I'm only teasing you. We're spending the night in here.**

(B) **Good, now stop teasing me. I always fall for it**

(S) **I will do that now go enjoy yourself too and don't write yourself off for tomorrow**

(B). **We will and I won't. I want to remember every minute of tomorrow.**

Well, that's the boys teased. Let's enjoy ourselves upstairs, Honey. I led Christa upstairs to my room. I opened the door, saying, "Ta-dah…" waving my hand around the door for her to enter my room.

"Wow, Sherry, you went to so much trouble for me. Thank you so much. I love it," while getting all teary. It must be my pregnancy hormones kicking in again.

"Ok, take a pew on my bed next to the snacks, and I'll load up the Mama Mia movie for us to watch. Unless you would like to watch something else?"

"No, that one's good," while I grabbed a handful of nuts and candy to stuff my mouth with. We watched the movie while giggling and talking about the movie. I fell asleep at some stage. Poor Sherry, it was in her bed, too. She left me there and slept in the bed she had set up for me.

Before I knew it, I was getting rudely awakened by Sherry. "Come on, Chick, it's time to shower. I've had mine. Then we can go down and have breakfast before that crew Brazen has organized to come in at ten to do our hair and makeup. Then it will be time to get your gorgeous dress on to blow that husband-to-be of yours away when he sees you in it."

"Yeah! Thanks Sherry" I sighed. I didn't want to get up. I was still tired but needed to get up and prepare for my big day. I got showered and dressed while Sherry went downstairs to make breakfast.

Chapter Twenty Five - Christa

Once I had showered and gone down for breakfast, chaos reigned. I just managed to eat my breakfast before the two ladies, Pam and Louisa, turned up to do our hair and makeup. I downed my coffee. Then I went and sat in one of the two chairs Sherry had set up in the kitchen for us to get our hair styled, followed by our makeup. When Louisa finished my make-up, she put the mirror up for me to see how I looked. "Oh gosh, I want to cry, but I'll ruin my makeup. Thank you; you've made me look more beautiful than I ever imagined I could." She had styled my long hair loose with lots of soft curls.

"No crying" she laughed. You will spoil your mascara, and I don't want to be redoing your makeup again. Now, I shall follow you upstairs and help you with your dress. Then, I shall attach your headpiece for you. "

"Okay." I spun around to leave my seat and saw Sherry was nearly finished. I almost didn't recognize her with her hair and makeup. Louisa followed me up the stairs to Sherry's bedroom. I opened the door and entered. I grabbed my dress, hanging over a rail in the closet, and placed it on the bed. I took my clothes off and stood in the corset and lacy G-string I had purchased to wow Brazen on our wedding night. I felt somewhat embarrassed at Louisa seeing me like this. She took the dress from the cover, helped me place it over my head, and zipped it up. She then toyed with my hair some more. She grabbed the veil headpiece off the bed and affixed it to my hair. I went and looked in the mirror, gasping, putting my hand over my mouth since I couldn't believe how beautiful I looked in my wedding dress.

The bedroom door opened again, and Sherry entered the room. "Wow, Sherry, you look amazing," I gasped.

"Thanks, Christa. But I don't look as stunning as you do in that dress. I told you that you would. Brazen will be gobsmacked when he sees you coming down the aisle. Now, I guess I better get my wedding gear on, too! That limousine should be arriving soon to take us to your fate," I winked at Christa. Pam helped me with my dress and put on my floral headpiece, and now we were both ready. I felt nervous myself. Goodness knows how Christa must be feeling. I heard a knock at the door. "Yes, " I called out.

"Sherry, it's only me, Sandra. I'm letting you know your car has arrived and is waiting downstairs."

"Thanks, Honey. Can you let him know we should be down in five minutes?" I grabbed the two champagne flutes I had set out on the nightstand, then grabbed the sparkling apple juice to fill them with and handed one to Christa. "I'll have to toast you with this since there is no alcohol for you, Miss. Cheers to you. I wish you and Brazen a long and happy life together," raising my glass to chink against Christa's glass.

"Thank you, Sherry. Me too," I blushed before sipping the apple juice.

"Come on then, Christa, we better get downstairs before the limo driver starts getting antsy because we're late. Though it's always good for the bride-to-be to be late, I say" giggling. We went downstairs, and the limo driver helped us with our dresses and rearranged them so we didn't get them too creased in the back. "Well, here we go, Christa. How are you feeling nervous?"

"Yes. I'm petrified, though I don't know why. I can't wait to get married to my amazing man. I'm starting to feel nauseous, too. I hope I can hang on to my breakfast." I mumbled.

"Me too! Yikes, that's all we need in the back of the limo if you lose your breakfast. I'm sure you'll be fine," reassuring her, patting the back of her hand. "Would you like some water? They also have water in the mini-fridge here with the champagne."

"Yes, I will give that a try. Thanks Sherry," I grabbed the bottle she handed me like it was a lifeline. I took a tentative sip, which made me feel mildly better. I took another small sip to calm my nerves and stomach. Before I knew it, we were pulling up to the compound's front gate. *Oh god, this is it now.* Hawk was guarding the entrance in a suit. He smiled and waved before opening the gate to let us pass through. We wound our way up the drive lined with white balloons. The boys had done a lovely job of making the place look like a wedding was happening. When we pulled up to the house's front door, there was a big banner with Brazen and Christa's Wedding and today's date. Aww, something we could keep for prosperity to remember our day.

"Wow, Brazen and Mo have thought of everything, haven't they?" I told Christa.

"Yes, more than I imagined they would do," I sighed. When we stopped, Mo came out the front door. He looked such a handsome sight in a suit. I elbowed Sherry. "Mo has gone all out for you, too. Sherry, he's even put on a suit."

"Shut up" I blushed. "He's doing it because it's your big day, and he's the best man for Brazen."

"Sure, keep telling yourself that woman. I see how he sometimes looks at you when he thinks no one is looking." I loved embarrassing my friend.

"Hush you, he does not," making me blush at the thought this handsome man would feel anything for me.

Mo opened the door to let me out, wolf-whistling when he saw me in my wedding dress. He helped me out of the car.

"Geez, Christa, you might make Brazen faint when he sees you. You look stunning in this dress."

I stood aside so he could help Sherry out of the car. He grabbed her hand to help her out of the car, but not before giving her a gentle kiss on the back of Sherry's hand, which made her blush beet red. I tried not to giggle at the sight before me. Once Sherry was out of the car, he led us both around the side of the house to the back garden, which had been set up for the event.

I was stunned when I saw the back garden when we rounded the corner. There was an archway filled with various all-white flowers, with another one down the other end of the 'aisle' for us to get married under. While white chairs covered in satin were laid out for all the guests to sit in. Mo and Christa went ahead of me down the aisle. While I followed close behind. I wondered if I should have invited my father to give me away on my big day. But that thought soon left my head. He would never have approved of my sexy, handsome man standing down the aisle with the wedding officiant who would be marrying us.

I blushed when the guests, consisting of the other men and their wives or girlfriends, clapped as I made my way down the aisle. I nodded to them while I made my way down to my waiting man, bouncing around on his feet with nervousness, waiting for me. He wanted to look but waited until I stood beside him to savor the moment. Mo and Sherry reached the end. I watched Mo kiss Sherry's cheek before taking his place next to Brazen while Sherry went to stand on the opposite side, waiting for me.

I reached them and took my place standing next to Brazen. When he saw me, he mouthed at me, "You look beautiful, baby," while his eyes started glistening with tears.

"Thank you handsome. You look amazing in your suit," I mouthed back.

Our marriage officiant welcomed all our guests and started saying the vows. Everything drowned out around me while I stared my Brazen in the eyes while he held my hands. He had to keep prompting me when it was my turn to repeat my vows. I was mesmerized by my man so much I couldn't take my eyes off his. I wondered if I might burst his bubble later with my secret. Before I knew it, we exchanged rings and were now Mr and Mrs Martinez. We went to the little table nearby to sit and sign the register while some music played for the other guests. Once all the official duties were out of the way, Mo advised our guests to go to the marquee at the end of the garden to have drinks and food while we had photos taken.

We could relax and join our guests once we had posed for our photos. Brazen grabbed my hand and dragged me to the marquee.

"Hey, slow down, husband. I have heels on, don't forget, and trying to walk on the grass here."

"Sorry baby. I want to get this out the way to have you all to myself. God, I thought I had died, and you were an angel sent to me, looking stunning in your beautiful dress. I love it."

"Thank you, Handsome. I like that look you're rocking in that suit. I need to see you in one more often," I giggled.

Once we reached the tent, I asked her, "champagne?"

"Ummm, err, no. I'll have an apple juice," I stuttered. I was nervous I still had to break my secret news to him.

"Apple juice," I glared at her. "You not feeling well, my love?" I put my hand across her forehead. No, that felt fine; it wasn't that. "Are you hungover?"

"No neither of those. How about we grab our drinks and sit somewhere private."

"Okay," staring quizzingly at her, wondering why we had to sit somewhere quiet for this tale. I grabbed a beer and an apple juice for my beautiful wife and sat down at the bridal table while everyone else was mixing and mingling. However, we were never going to get quiet in here. "Well, break it to me gently, baby. I don't know how many more surprises I can take today." I grumbled.

"Okay," though I was still nervous about what I would tell him. I grabbed his hand and held it in mine while rubbing my thumb over the back of his hands. "Ummm, I wanted to let you know that I can't drink because you're going to become a daddy," I told him while absentmindedly brushing invisible pieces of lint off his suit jacket.

I stood immediately after yelling, "WHAT." I was immediately sorry for my overreaction when I saw her happy face crumble, and her lip began to tremble as a silent tear left her eye. Now, I had caused a scene. All the guests were looking our way, wondering what was happening. They waited, embarrassed while waiting and wondering what to do next. "It's okay, folks, carry on." I sat back down again, pulled her into my arms, and sat her on my lap. "I'm sorry, gorgeous," rubbing my hand through her hair to reassure her. "I didn't mean to scare you. Oh my god, I love you. I can't believe we're going to have a baby. You have made me happy for the second time today. First, you agree to marry me, and then tell me we're having a baby. Oh god, is it okay if I tell everyone? I must tell someone before I explode. I may as well tell everyone. Sorry, I overreacted. I was shocked before I got excited about the thought."

"Yeah. I'm glad we're having a baby to seal our love."

I stood up, excitement and happiness overwhelming me. "Would everyone please raise your glasses? I'm pleased to tell you that not only did we get married today. But my beautiful wife has just told me we're expecting a baby." I was ecstatic when the place exploded in cheers and whistles, happy for us both. I raised my glass and took a sip before sitting down next to my wife. "I know we should mix and mingle with our guests. But I want to sit beside you and never leave your side, baby. You've made me so happy. I never thought in my whole life that I would ever have a child. Now, here you've made all my wishes come true in one day." I pulled her closer and kissed her deep and hard on the lips. I felt a tap on my shoulder, and I moaned. "What" I cursed "fuck" when I saw it was Mo. "What do you want?"

"Well, I came to wish you congratulations. I'm so happy for you both. But now I'm only happy for Christa," he glared. "Plus, you need to get a room if you want to carry on with your porn show in front of your guests."

"Sorry, Mo, I just caught up in the moment and forgot what I was doing, and I'm happy we're having a baby. I didn't mean to snap at you. Thanks. Plus, thank you for being my best man and doing a great job with all the planning and wonderful job you've done putting our big day together at short notice."

"Apology accepted. I'm pleased for you both with the little one on the way," slapping Brazen on the back. I leaned over and whispered in his ear, "You will have to keep her close to you and safe. I hope word doesn't get out to put you both in danger."

"I know. Thanks." I was worried, too, about what would happen if word got out about some of the drama we had run into of late."

"Okay that said Brazen. You two enjoy the rest of your day now," slapping his shoulder as I left. It's time to search for that little minx Sherry I had my eye on. But I don't want anyone to know, of course. I better not forget to do my best man duties later when the caterers are ready to serve the wedding dinner. What you can do on short notice is impressive when you offer to pay double or triple for their service. Aah, there's my little minx over there chatting to some ladies. I shall interrupt her fun. "Ladies," I nodded at them all, causing them to giggle. Still got that charm, older man, I thought to myself. Sherry didn't seem quite as impressed. She rolled her eyes. I'll soon stop that attitude. "Sorry ladies, I must steal Sherry from you all for more of her wedding duties."

I glared at him. *What the fuck was he on about? Wedding duties? We had already done those as far as I knew, apart from our speeches during the wedding meal.* "What wedding duties might those be, Mo?" I demanded.

"Time to come sort those two out and get everyone together to eat. Follow me, darlin'."

I eyed him suspiciously. "Okay," while I followed him over to the bridal table. I was still eyeing him suspiciously with his intentions.

I didn't know what to do with her now that I had her. My bravado had disappeared the longer she walked beside me towards Brazen and Christa at the bridal table. Both were still reveling in their happy news. I put my hand along her lower back to test the waters. But it was soon brushed away with an indignant huff on her part. Okay, maybe I'm moving too fast. Fuck I hadn't felt like I ever needed another woman until now... But it seemed like it wasn't reciprocated. I need to give her more time to get used to me. I was saved by the caterers starting to come in with the food and placing it on the tables for people to serve themselves. We would be served separately at the bridal table.

I wolf-whistled to attract everyone's attention. "Okay, thank you, everyone, for coming to celebrate Brazen and Christa's nuptials. Please help yourself to a meal and find a table to sit at. I grabbed Christa's hand, pulling her behind me and seating her next to me at the bridal table before she could complain. "We just need to stay here, everyone. The caterers will serve us here at the bridal table. I'll get them to give us a bottle of apple juice for you, Christa; now you can't drink alcohol. You will need a drink to toast with." I smiled. "We don't want you to feel left out at your wedding."

Chapter Twenty Six - Brazen & Christa

The rest of the wedding dinner went without incident, and I think everyone had a great time. We had to leave early since I was starting to get tired. It was such a big, exciting day, and I had the best time ever. I was exhausted but happily married, and Brazen was pleased with a baby coming, too. Best wedding present ever, he assured me. I don't think I will ever wipe that grin off his face. It's stuck there permanently now. We weren't going away on a honeymoon. We decided to stay home. But now that we had a baby on the way, we decided to go somewhere for a break before we had our baby.

Although I was tired, Brazen managed to wake my body up with his kisses and other things he did to me to consummate our marriage. He picked me up and carried me over the threshold of our bedroom and sat me with care down on our bed. He unzipped my gown and helped me get it off. His eyes bugged out of his head when he saw the lingerie I had on under there.

"Fuck baby, what are you trying to do to me here with that sexy lingerie. My cock has gone instantly hard" while I'm trying desperately to readjust myself in my pants but failing miserably. "Fuck it off, they come," I told my shoes off and sat down to take my socks off, tossing them away. I stood up, unzipping my pants and tossing them aside. I struggled with my tie but eventually got that off, too. I didn't care about the shirt and just ripped it down, the middle buttons flying off everywhere.

"You horny or something, husband?" I giggled at his antics to get undressed in a hurry.

"Ya think, baby. I can't wait to feel my cock in that sweet wet tight pussy of yours. I need to feel it gripping my cock. I'll get to you in a minute, trust me." Finally, when I got my shirt off, I walked over to my gorgeous new wife with my cock bobbing proudly around. Now to get these panties off so I can get to that dripping pussy and quench my thirst. I gripped them and ripped them off in my haste. I pushed her down and knelt on the bed between her legs. I threw her legs over my shoulders and bent down, licking her pussy, and sucking her clit in between breaths. I sat up and began rubbing her clit and banging my hard cock across her pussy. She was close. I could feel it when her legs began to shake before she came gushing everywhere all over me. Oh, yessss, I fist pumped. "I love how you're a squirter, baby." I began rubbing her clit. "Turn over, baby. I want to take you from behind. Now hurry, please. I don't know how much longer I can last, Baby."

I moaned about having to move from being comfy lying on the bed. "Awww, I was comfy lying on my back too." I reluctantly turned over and got on all fours. He made me groan when he began rubbing my clit, sending shivers through my body. It felt so amazing with all the sensations he was giving me.

"I'm coming in now, baby. Prepare yourself. I'll try to be gentle since I don't want to hurt the baby."

"I don't think you'll hurt the baby yet, handsome. It'll be just a blip on the radar and plenty of protection. Now hurry, I need to cum again. You're making me very horny with all you do and say. Oh, fuck when he stilled and began pumping his cum in me, hitting all the right spots. I came gripping his cock tight. I could feel the vein still pumping his cum out deep in me." I sighed and collapsed on the bed with exhaustion, rolling over and looking him deep in the eyes. "That's enough, handsome. I don't think I can take any more tonight. I'm exhausted."

"Yeah, I'm done too. I hope you enjoyed your wedding day. I know I did, and the incredible blessing we have with a baby on the way. I hope I'm a good dad.

"Course you will. We'll both be learning how to be parents. After all, babies don't come with instructions" I smiled poking his chest. "I know you will be a good dad to our baby jellybean. You're a kind, caring man to those you love."

I sighed. "I hope so baby." I lay back on the bed with my right hand behind my head, looking up at the ceiling, wondering whether our baby would be a boy or a girl. I wrapped my arm around her, bringing her head over my chest and kissing her forehead. "Night baby, sweet dreams," I rubbed circles around her belly while listening to her soft snores while she slept. I eventually drifted off to sleep.

Morning came around too soon. We had forgotten to close the curtains the night before, and now the morning sun shone through, making the bedroom bright. I groaned and slowly extricated myself from a still-sleeping Christa lying across my right arm. I headed to the bathroom to do my morning business before showering. I got dressed and headed downstairs for my morning heart starter and coffee. I made my coffee and headed out onto the veranda for the first smoke of the day. I grabbed my packet and lighter out of the pot on the table and lit my smoke, taking the first drag for the day. God, it felt good. Now might be a good time to give them up with our baby on the way. At the same time, I was enjoying the morning peace and trying not to look at the mess littering the back garden from the night before. It looked like it had gone on until the wee small hours, but at least they had kept quiet since they never disturbed Christa or me. I heard the kitchen door to the veranda open, and Mo appeared.

"Well, you look like shit. You must have had a great night. What time did you pack it in?" I enquired.

"I'm not traveling too bad. I headed up to bed at about 3 a.m. Sorry about the mess. I'll get the men onto it later when they surface. Some of them were still kicking on when I went to bed."

"That's okay so long as someone cleans it all up. Thanks for all your help organizing and helping me plan the wedding, Mo."

"You're welcome. You two deserve to belong to each other, and I'm glad you both found each other and now you're expecting a baby. Maybe you better give them smokes up with a baby on the way."

"I know I was just thinking that myself. Once I've finished this packet, I'll give them up. I'll only smoke out here and not around Christa. I never thought I'd be destined to get married, let alone have a child."

"Well, life is full of surprises. You never know what is waiting around the corner."

"Now you just need to find your forever Mo. I think you deserve it. What about Sherry? You both seem to get along well, especially in yesterday's roles."

"Oh hell no Brazen! I'm never getting married. I settled down once but never again. I got badly burned and vowed never again would I get in a relationship with a woman."

"Well, sounds like there's a story there," I mused.

"One day, but not now. I may never reveal my past to anyone," I retorted. "Anyways I heard a whisper on the grapevine..." I was determined to change the subject away from my love life or lack thereof in that department.

"Oh," my ears prick up with excitement with that piece of information. "Do tell me."

"I hear a whisper on the grapevine that Torres thinks we stole his backup hard drive when we took those women. Now I know we didn't take anything apart from those women from that place. I trust that none of our men did either. What do you think? Are we being wrongly blamed? Or do you think maybe one of our men did take it? Or maybe one of those men we left in the basement for Torres and his other men to find stole it? I know so many questions and no answers," I observed.

"I think we can trust our men. I'll call for church when everyone is awake and ask them. I'll advise them to be honest if they did take his property. We want to know for our safety and theirs and to be honest. They won't be in trouble with us. Should any of our men here have it, we want to know what's on it. Otherwise, if no one owns up, we can assume Torres has lost it and blamed us for saving grace, or one of his men took it. Either way, we need to know and take the appropriate action."

"Yep, sounds like a good plan. I think I'll have something to eat. Do you want something to eat? I'll heat some of the leftovers, nothing fancy."

"Yeah, I will. I'm starting to feel hungry too. I'll take some up to Christa after. I better keep my woman fed since she must eat for two now," I grinned.

I slapped Brazen on the back. "Yeah, you need to look after her even more now, Braze." I went into the kitchen and pulled a variety of leftovers out, plating up two plates, heating them in the microwave, and taking them over to the table where Brazen sat waiting. "Here ya go, help yourself to what you want." We sat eating and deep in our thoughts.

"Whelp, that's me stuffed now," I said, leaning back in my chair and patting my stomach. I guess I better feed the little lady now if she's awake." I laughed when Mo shook his head and rolled his eyes at me. I grabbed another plate from the cupboard, put some food on the plate for Christa, and heated it before taking it upstairs. I opened the door and saw she was lying there awake. "Morning, my gorgeous wife. How are you feeling this morning?"

"Mmmm..." I said while stretching. "I'm good. I feel a bit nauseous. But now I'm hungry, smelling that food," moving to sit in bed. "Thank you, handsome," when he placed the tray on my lap. "Would you like some?"

"No thanks, gorgeous. I've just eaten some. I didn't want to disturb you in case you were still sleeping. But I see you're not," bending down to kiss her on the cheek. I sat on the bed beside her, wrapping my arm around her shoulders. "Would you like to do anything later? I'll call church early in the afternoon about some intel Mo has found. But after that, I hope to be free."

"I'd just like a lazy day around the home, maybe reading. It will be good to sit and do nothing for a change after all the hectic activity preparing for the wedding over the past few days."

"You've got it. I'll come and join you there when I can after my meeting. I better wake these men still sleeping so they can clear all the rubbish from the back lawn first. They left after the wedding instead of clearing up after the celebrations. It will all need to be done before we have church."

"Okay, thank you for the food, and I'll see you later." I smiled. I felt like the luckiest woman in the whole wide world, married to my amazing hubby.

I went downstairs in search of Mo. I found him still sitting at the kitchen table when I went downstairs. "Come on, let's get these men up. They've had long enough to sleep. If they haven't well too bad. We need to get the back garden cleaned up before we meet before we call our church meeting."

"Agreed," pushing my chair back and heading towards the men's quarters, banging on their doors as I went, "everybody up now." I grinned when I heard a few complaints behind the doors. "Time to eat before cleaning up. Then we have church. Urgent business. Get your asses into gear. I can tell you if I need to come and get anyone out of bed, it won't be a pretty sight. Everyone up now." I headed back down to the kitchen to wait. I felt pleased with myself when the men slowly filed into the kitchen, moaning with their hangovers. "Afternoon, all. Grab yourselves some leftovers. When you've eaten, we shall head out into the back garden to clean up. Therefore, take a garbage bag with you. We will call church once the garden is cleaned to my satisfaction."

Once the men finished their brunch with a lot of moaning and groaning, they followed me into the garden. Once the garden was cleared of rubbish, we stacked it in the dumpster. We stopped in the kitchen for drinks, then carried onto the basement for Brazen to hold church.

"Welcome, everyone, and thanks for tidying up the garden. I hope everyone had a great time yesterday." I smiled when everyone nodded and showed their appreciation for being a part of our wedding. "It has come to our attention that Torres has blamed us for 'stealing a hard drive' from his property when we rescued the women. Mo and I know that we didn't take it." Abruptly there was, an uproar erupted from the men around the table. I raised my arms. "Hang on, I am not blaming my men for doing so. I would like to know if anyone did take it at the time. "You won't be in trouble with Mo or me. But if someone has the alleged stolen item, we would like to see what data it contains. If no one has it, the problem is solved, and we must clear our name. He could be blaming us to stir trouble against us. Mo and I will sort it out if no one here has the alleged stolen item. Okay then. Now, does anyone have any more business to discuss?" Silence reigned. "Okay, the meeting is now closed. You're free for the rest of the day unless you are rostered on for duties on the compound."

Only Mo and I left when all the men had left the room. "What do you think we call Torres's bluff?"

"Yep! We don't have it. He or one of his men must have it. I'll drop the word in the right circles: he's tripping that we had nothing to do with the theft. If that's all, Braze, I'll take myself for a ride."

"Nope. You're free to do whatever you wish. I'll be here looking after the little woman and any problems that crop up. Enjoy yourself and take care out there."

Chapter Twenty Seven – Six Months Later
Brazen & Christa

I bailed Brazen up at breakfast. "I need to see you in your office now. It's urgent."

"Okay. I'm coming now to lead the way. What's up?" concerned what this was about.

"When we're in your office, I told you." I glared at Brazen over my shoulder.

"Okay, okay. You forgot to mention top secret business while you were at it, Mo" getting short with him. I was glad when we reached my office to find out what this was all about.

I sat heavily in the chair opposite Brazen's desk while I waited for him to get seated in his chair. "Well, we need to go to our other warehouse interstate. Word is Torres is about to raid our warehouse there and steal our stock.'

"Like hell is he' slamming my hands down on my desk and standing up while pacing behind my desk. "We'll round all the men up and take the van. I wouldn't say I like leaving Christa alone, but I must come. Just in case, we'll leave a few men behind to protect her. But if he's raiding our property there, we don't need to worry about him coming here. Do you reckon it's a legitimate threat what he's doing or a distraction?"

"Word on the street, it's legitimate for us stealing his hard drive and his women that we stole. He's doing it tough with those losses. This is his retaliation to steal product from us and make us pay."

"Hmmm... okay, if you're sure, get the van and the men ready while I go and tell Christa the bad news." Much as it pained me to leave her here by herself, being the president had its disadvantages at times. I sighed, feeling my heart fall to the pit of my stomach with what I had to do. I watched Mo leave my office while I gathered the momentum and courage to tell my wife the bad news. Right, it's now or never. I tried to convince myself, but I did not feel it.

I walked into the bedroom, searching for my gorgeous girl. I was not looking forward to breaking the bad news to her. I found her lying down on the bed, reading. I sat on the bed beside her, kissing her hard on her sweet, luscious full lips. "Hey, Babe, how are you feeling?"

"Tired but positive. I will be better when I have this baby. Now, why do I feel that you're preparing me for bad news?" glancing over at him with a frown.

I swallowed a lump in my throat when I saw her frown. I felt incredibly guilty enough as it was for leaving her here alone. "Yeah, about that. I'm sorry, I must go out of town for a few days." I stretched my arms around her as best I could with her pregnant baby bump, the only thing separating us these days. I kissed her face and the side of her neck, nuzzling my nose in her neck to smell her vanilla scent. "I'm so sorry, Baby I hate to be away from you in your condition, but this time I have no choice...."

"Are you trying to butter me up by smothering me in kisses here, Handsome?"

"You're onto me, aren't you." I sighed, "You know me too well. Business, you know how it is. I hate when it takes me away from you. I'll have to take a few of my men with me. I'll leave three of my best men to stay and protect you while I'm gone. I'm not expecting any trouble, just erring on caution, Babe." *I was being cautious. I wasn't expecting anything to happen, but who knows when you have enemies these days? Always wait for that moment when you slip up, and then they strike when you're vulnerable. No matter how much you keep your ear to the ground.* "I must protect you and our little peanut while I'm gone," I said, placing my hands on her belly, feeling our little peanut moving around. *She knows when her daddy is nearby.*

"I know. This is your life. I accept it since I want to be with you. But it's still hard, and that doesn't mean I have to like it," she sniffed.

"Hey, hey, hey, Gorgeous. Please don't cry." I grabbed her by the cheeks, tipping her head up to gaze lovingly into her eyes.

"I worry about you while you're gone, too. Will this be the time he doesn't come back? Will I be a single mom bringing up our baby? I always stress that something will happen to you whenever you leave the house on business. I think I'll never see you again," tears pouring over her eyes and dripping down her cheeks. "Sorry, it's the hormones, you know."

"Hey, those hormones are fine to have, Baby. I'll be okay. I promise. I have men who have my back with me. Torres has been up to no good again. I was positive now that I've got him back on my radar. We need to stop him and his trafficking. I'll come back to you; I promise."

"Okay," I sniffed. Then, I pulled his head down and kissed him hard like it was the last time I would ever see him. I could feel it in my gut. "Please keep safe and return to me and our baby peanut Brazen. Please promise me."

I wrapped my arms around her, holding her tight and never wanting to let her go. "I wish I could take you with me, gorgeous. But it's far too dangerous," I sighed.

"I know. But I can still worry about you and miss you while you're gone. You are the love of my life, handsome."

"I'll be as quick as I can. I'll try to get back early if we can. I wouldn't say I like leaving you alone here. If anything happens to you or the baby, I'm not here to help you."

"We will be fine. Stop worrying, baby. I still have two months to go. But you better hurry up and put that furniture together in the nursery for me before Peanut comes along. I don't want to have to remind you again."

I laughed. "Yeah, I'm sorry. Time is getting away from me, huh!" I smiled when she slapped me on the arm, telling me...

"Yes, it is. You better get on to that when you get back..."

"Oh, threatening me now, huh!" I couldn't help but smile at her. "I need to go now, gorgeous," slapping her ass. "We're heading off shortly. I'll be back as soon as I can. I'll hopefully only be away for one night or two at the most. I'll ring you and let you know if we need to be away for two nights."

"You better, or there will be hell to pay when you return."

I held my hands up in mock terror. "Oh, my god. I'm going now. You're getting brutal towards me now." I gave her one final hug. "I love you, baby. Hell, I will miss you like crazy while I'm gone." I rubbed her stomach again, feeling our baby move beneath my hand. "You know your daddy, don't you, peanut? Please care for our peanut while I'm gone, Babe."

"You know I will. But we need a new nickname since our peanut is a bit bigger than a peanut now, with two months to go. Love you. Please come back to me. I don't know what to do if you never return to me."

"I promise. Come 'ere," pulling her towards me and kissing her hard. I didn't want to leave her here, but duty called. When I finally broke for air, "Bye, babe," I whispered. "I'll see you soon," tapping her on the tip of her nose. "Let me see," tapping my finger on my chin, feigning I was deep in thought. "Our new nickname for our little one should be pumpkin Since they are about that size now. I promise I'll return." Again, I kissed my finger and tapped her on the nose.

I walked away from her, full of regret and helplessness, walking out the door. Ready but unwilling to join Mo and the other men in our van waiting out the front. I hated leaving her behind in her current condition. But my hands are bound at times when business calls. I was the Prez and needed to go with my men. We had to deal with Torres' shit once and for all. I got in the passenger seat. "Okay, let's get on our way and hit the road, Mo." We drove down my drive, getting shaken around while we drove down the gravel drive to the main highway.

Chapter Twenty Eight - Brazen

After driving for seven hours, we finally got to the warehouse we shared with the Diamonds. It all seemed too quiet like nothing had happened here earlier, which made me wonder if this was a setup. Were we going to be attacked by someone now that we were here? Or, while we were blissfully unaware, clearing up the mess left around here. Boxes had been opened, and their contents were tossed everywhere. Would they strike, then? Something in my gut didn't feel right about what was happening here.

A couple of my men who had been here guarding the warehouse for the Diamonds were getting checked out by Doc. He shook his head no in my direction. Fuck it, two good men taken down cut across the throats. It appeared they had been outnumbered by whoever came to steal from us. They hadn't seemed successful. Alternatively, they wanted to leave us a message. I would have to put my ear to the ground along with Mo sniffing around to see who was behind this. Things had been quiet of late, so this was unexpected. We were working with everyone, so unless one of them had decided to double-cross us, I had no idea what was happening here. Something told me Torres was back in town and had an axe to grind. We needed to find out where he was hiding out. "This smells like something Torres would do."

Mo stood there scratching his chin, looking at me. "I dunno. But this seems too staged to me. Do you think this was a setup?"

"It does seem odd that our men were killed, especially when the Diamonds are working with us. Fuck I bet it was a distraction to get us away from the house. Christa's there alone with only a few men for protection, and we're all here, miles away. Fuck" punching a wall with my fist. *Fuck that hurt.* I pulled my phone out of my pocket and rang security at the gate. "Come on, hurry up and answer fuckers" breathing a sigh of relief that I didn't realize I was holding when someone finally answered. "Mile's it's me. Thank fuck you answered. Be on the lookout. It might be a setup up for this call-out. We're too far away to get back there in time. Can you get some more backup in from somewhere if you can? I want everyone to be safe, especially with Christa alone without me for protection."

"Gotcha! I'll call some of our Stoner pals in to help. They owe us a big favor."

"Thanks, I appreciate it. I hope I'm wrong, but... We'll finish up here, and then we'll be back as soon as possible."

"Ok, Prez. I'll get more backup and keep you updated."

"Good, and don't forget to keep me updated, either" I said, hanging up my phone. I turned to Mo. "What do you reckon? Wrap it up here now and find out what the fuck is going on. It's beginning to stink more and more that I think about it. It's beginning to smell like a setup to draw us away from the compound. But why?"

"Yeah, it smells to me, too. Who, I have no idea. I haven't heard any whispers in the wind about anyone wanting revenge on us. But I can put the word out there and see if we get anything back."

"Do that then," I ordered back. "Come on, men, wrap it up. Apart from a plot to get us away from the compound, there is nothing to see here. Let's get back and find out what's going on here." I wandered over to where Doc was placing some blankets over the two dead men, Ginger and Spike. "I'll send out a clean-up crew later to sort out his mess for us, Doc," I patted him on the shoulder.

"Yeah, at least they didn't suffer.

"Hey, Mo," I called. "Doc is nearly finished. Until we know what's going on, we all go back. We do have cameras to keep an eye on the place. We're far away, and they'll be gone before we get here. But at least we will have proof of who it is and what they're doing. We'll look back later at the footage and see if we can make out who it is from the footage."

"Yeah, that's good. Who knows, maybe they might go through with more next time if we leave our people here since today's attack was a warning for us. Until we know who and what we should keep away." Once everyone was ready, we hit the highway and headed out with the men to visit our new contact, Gonzales. Whom we were hoping to set up as a new product supplier.

Chapter Twenty Nine - Brazen

We had an uneventful ride out to meet our new contact. Whom we hoped would use our services as a new supplier. I felt guilty at the fact that I had to leave Christa behind. I was especially seeing she was so far along in her pregnancy. But my hands were tied. I was the Prez and needed to come along. Any visits in the future wouldn't matter as much. I could send Mo as my second in command, but I needed to be here today for the first visit. I felt relieved when we entered the compound without incident. Meeting with anyone new is always a bit dicey since you never know in our line of business if they might be double-crossing you. We were granted entry after checking out our credentials. We pulled up near the compound entrance, ready to meet our new head buyer, Gonzales.

He came out the door, inviting us in and leading us down the hallway to his office. We followed, checking out the place as we went in case, we needed to escape in a hurry should anything happen. Gonzales sat down in his chair behind the desk, leaning back in his chair. He gestured for us to sit in the two chairs before his desk. "Welcome, Brazen and Mo'. You're looking for some new product, I hear. What are you looking for, and in what quantities? Then we can discuss the price.

"Marijuana is the only item I deal in. We're looking at 100 pounds monthly. What can you offer?" I watched Gonzales figure it up with his fingers steepled at his chin.

"Hmmm... let us say $100 grand," raising his eyebrows while awaiting my response across from his desk.

"What about $90k? How does that sound?" I knew I was pushing my luck, but he could only say yes or no to that amount.

"$96k, and we have a deal."

I responded, "done," while getting up and half sitting out of my chair and reaching across to shake hands on the deal.

I reached over and grabbed Brazen's hand, shaking it in mine. "Done deal. I can't interest you in any weapons?"

"Nah. Not at this stage, anyway. If we do in the future, I'll know where to come," I winked. "Now, are you sending me an invoice to pay? Or cut you a cheque now?" I grinned when Gonzales raised his eyebrows at me. "I know, I know. Want the cash now or on delivery?"

"Preferably before delivery. But since this is our first transaction. Then you know that you can trust me and my product. I'll allow payment in cash, of course, on product delivery. But in the future, it will be before delivery."

"Thank you for your trust, Gonzales, and it's a pleasure doing business with you. If you ever need anything or help in any way. Please don't hesitate to contact me," I assured him.'

"Noted. It is a pleasure doing business with you, Brazen, and you won't be disappointed. Would you like a scotch to celebrate?"

"Maybe just a small one since we have a long ride home again. Plus, I don't want to be too long. I've left my pregnant wife at home."

"I can imagine. Congratulations, we do need one to toast the future arrival." I turned behind me, grabbing three shot glasses and my best whisky for my new client. I placed the glasses down on my desk and filled them. I pushed two glasses towards them and picked up mine, ready to toast. "Here's to our new business venture and your imminent arrival to your family. Cheers…"

"Thanks. Cheers. Here's to new beginnings…" I downed mine and reflected, "aah that's a delicious drop." It was the best shot I had ever tasted, and I placed my glass on Gonzales's desk. "Sorry, this is a rushed visit. But we can't stay longer. We need to be heading back home." I was worried about Christa at home alone and if something would happen to her while we were gone.

"That's understandable. I'll drop by when we come with the first shipment. Give me two weeks."

"Certainly. Until then, it's been a pleasure doing business with you, Gonzales." Mo and I turned to leave his office.

"I'll come and see you both out." I walked around my desk, opened the door, and led the way down to the front door. I opened it when we arrived and shook their hands on their way out. "Bye, see you in a few." I nodded.

"Bye," chorused Mo and me while we walked to our bikes. We had left our other men out the front waiting since only Mo and I needed to be in the meeting with Gonzales. We started them up, went down the long drive, and turned onto the highway on our way back. We were initially going to stay overnight due to Gonzales being a seven-hour drive from our compound. Also, we might have to conduct other business on the way back. But that was all up in the air since we needed to hurry home.

But in place of the threat from Torres, I needed to be home as soon as possible. I tried not to worry about things the whole drive back, which was impossible since I was doing anything but. But at least we struck no problems on our ride. We had to stop a couple of times for a pit stop or grab some food to keep us going.

I felt relieved when I saw my compound on the horizon. *Thank God. I'm nearly home baby.* I knew it was late, and she would probably be asleep. But I couldn't wait to jump into bed and hold her in bed. Had I known what fate awaited...

Chapter Thirty - Christa

I hate being by myself, especially in my current condition. I'm worried in case our pumpkin comes early when Brazen is away. I know first babies are usually late, but knowing my luck, this one will come early. I was feeling uneasy in my gut that something would go wrong this time while he was away. I worry that this time is the time that he won't come home. I went to do some more decorating in the nursery and put some wall stickers up. I needed to do something easy that didn't take much thinking today. I bought some bedding and sheets in white with a fern leaf design on them. I wanted unisex bedding because we want to get surprised when our baby comes along. I'll put them on to wash first; then, they're fresh and ready to put on the bed when our little pumpkin comes along. Once I've taken them out of the packaging and put them on to wash, I head upstairs to the nursery.

I picked up the wall stickers. They are so cute that they bring tears to my eyes with these stupid pregnancy hormones. I can't wait until our baby comes. I picked a variety, so we have some cute zoo animals, lions, giraffes, and rhinos. They also come with butterflies and clouds to go with the set. I decide what pattern I will do on the wall before sticking them. Once done, I stand back and observe my work on the wall. I'm pleased with how I have them spread over the wall, brightening the nursery up a bit. It was brilliant. It was all coming together, even if I only stuck them on the wall. I had the bassinet ready for Pumpkin and the matching nappy change table. I liked my nursing rocking chair and sat in it for another test drive.

Even though I hadn't done much, it was exhausting, and now that I had sat down... I felt tired. I glanced at my watch and saw it was 2 p.m. I went to lie down for my afternoon nap. I wandered down to our bedroom and sighed at the relief, taking the weight off my feet. Followed by bliss as I sank onto the mattress. Before I knew it, sleep took over. I smiled when I felt pumpkin moving in my belly. I put my hands over my stomach to protect our pumpkin, feeling them moving. I smiled while I watched and felt pumpkin somersault in my belly. "Not long now, only a couple more months. Before we get to see you and enjoy you in our life, pumpkin," I whispered. I began drifting off to sleep as exhaustion overtook me.

I woke up startled by a noise that disturbed my slumber. What was that noise? Omg, was that gunfire I heard? Then I heard what sounded like another shot fired. I could feel my heart pounding with fear for Pumpkin and me. What was going on? Oh god, where had I left my cell phone? I couldn't even remember. I raised myself and tried to get off the bed. Where could I hide in my current condition? The closet was my only option, and I waddled into the closet. I slid down the wall before flopping down onto the floor. I hid in the corner, anticipating the clothes would hopefully be enough to hide me. But I didn't feel hopeful. Hopefully, whoever it is isn't thorough enough to check the closets. *Where are you, Brazen? Can you hear me? I need you. Please help save Pumpkin and me. I don't know what's going on, and what I need you to do is keep us.* I screamed in my head to no avail. He was miles away and knew there was no saving us. I was scared but was resigned to my fate. Our men who stayed to guard me were outnumbered and had lost their lives, and I was now on my own.

I could still hear gunshots blazing outside. I put my hands over my ears to drown them out. I was starting to panic and didn't want a full-blown panic attack. I didn't want to alert the enemy to my hiding place. I hoped our guards could overcome whatever danger was happening outside. Petrified now, I was starting to shake in fear. Brazen only left three guards. Would they be enough to fight this enemy trying to invade our property? Where was Brazen? Why wasn't he here for me? Did he know this was happening? Was he coming back to save me? I couldn't hear any more gunfire. Everything was silent now. Was it all over now? Who had the upper hand now, our men or the intruders?

I would stay put and hoped they didn't enter the house. I expected the doors were all locked and I would be safe. I gasped, fear crawling down my spine when I heard the front door getting kicked in. This was not going to be good for me. It seemed locked doors weren't going to stop them. Whomever it was, they had now entered the house. I was now in extreme danger of that, I was sure. I needed to be strong and brave to protect myself and our baby. I had to sit tight here and hoped they wouldn't find me. I tried to squeeze in the corner as much as possible. I was anticipating the clothes would hide me, and they wouldn't see me if they checked in here.

I could hear them going through the house, opening doors, and trashing rooms. What were they searching for? I didn't know. Why did Brazen have to be gone and not be here to protect us? Nooo... Now, I could hear them coming up the stairs. They appeared to have finished doing their damage downstairs. I pulled my legs up under me the best I could with my belly in the way these days. I sat back and waited. My heart was pounding in my chest. I was praying to God that they wouldn't find me. I could hear them going through the other rooms on this level. I waited. I knew they would be in my room soon. Our bedroom was the last one down the hallway, so it would be the last place they had to check. I could hear them in Pumpkin's room, tossing the little furniture around. I felt the tears pricking my eyes. All our arduous work putting the room together was ruined in one fell swoop.

Chapter Thirty One - Christa & Torres

My breath caught when I could hear them outside my door. My heart is pounding in fear in my chest. They were here. Would I be safe? I listened to them going through the drawers in the bedroom and throwing items around. What were they searching for? Were we being robbed? Or did Brazen have something hidden that they wanted? Were they here wanting to trash our house because they felt it warranted intruding here in our house? I tried to remain still and quiet.

I jumped with a start when I heard the closet door open. I could listen to them as they started throwing our jewelry out of the cabinet in the middle of the walk-in closet. All I could hear was our watches, bracelets, necklaces, and rings flying and hitting the wall. I shut my eyes tight. I don't know what I was trying to achieve. I was beginning to shut down, and if I couldn't see them, they couldn't see me. Who knows? I tried hard not to jump whenever something hit the wall near my hiding place. I didn't want to give my hiding place away. I was hoping and praying they wouldn't find me here. I feared what they would do to me if or when they found me hiding in the closet.

I was sure now they were going to find me. They had started ripping our clothes off the hangers and tossing them on the floor. I kept my eyes shut tight and my hands over my ears. If I can't see them, they can't see me right. I felt a breeze whisper against my face when I felt the clothes in front of me ripped off the rail. Now, it appeared lighter where I was hiding. Now, the clothes no longer hid me.

Then I heard the voice I never hoped to hear ever again. *Oh fuck!* I cringed in fear, wishing I could roll myself up in a ball. It was virtually an impossible task now that I was pregnant. I was so fucked now. I would directly pay for Brazen taking me and the other women. I could feel it in my bones.

"Well, well, well, what do we have here? Hmmm, it's my little pet that got stolen from me," I spat out in disgust. "My, my, you and that asshole have been busy, haven't you." I glanced at her with a look of disgust written across my face. "I wasn't expecting to see this when I found my pet again. You are full of that devil's spawn," I said scathingly, repulsed with the vision in front of me now. "It should be you full of my baby in you, not his."

I screamed when he grabbed hold of my hair, pulling me up from the floor. I feared what he might do to me next. I was surprised at his strength. First, he could pull me up and my belly full of my baby with little effort. He pulled me back against his fat belly, licking my ear and making me cringe while a shiver ran down my spine.

"Hmmm... I see you shivering with excitement to see me, my little pet. Not so little anymore are you with that belly. What will I do with you, my little pet?" I whispered in her ear. I gave her ear a long lick. "Mmmm, yummy." She still tasted as delicious as I remembered. I felt my cock engorging with blood and poking her ass. "You want to feel my cock choking you and pounding that sweet tight pussy of yours." God, I wanted to shove my hard cock in her ass and relieve my hard-on. Fuck her deep and hard with no lube to punish her for what she has done. But instead, I pulled my gun out of its holster, pressing it against her belly. I rubbed the tip up and down her belly, laughing while she squirmed under my grip, begging me...

"Please don't hurt my baby and me, Torres. Please." I pleaded. "I'll do anything you want. Leave my baby alone." I sobbed in terror. I was terrified of what he might do to me.

"What makes you think I want you anymore? Observing you with this belly full of his devil's spawn. It disgusts me. This should be mine, not his." I poked it hard in her belly, making her jump. Once again, I began rubbing my gun against her stomach. I was so angry that he had taken her from me. Then fucked her until she was pregnant. She was always mine; now, he had ruined her for me. If I couldn't make her mine, no one would have her.

"P-p-p-please," I begged. "Don't hurt us. Let me go," I begged and prayed for mercy from him. He was soulless, and I knew no amount of begging would ever change his mind. All I could do was try. "Please don't Torres. What can I do to fix this?" I pleaded, praying for our lives. I had a fear it would be to no avail. His purpose now was probably to kill me. I sucked in a breath and closed my eyes, waiting for the inevitable, which I hoped wouldn't come, but I knew him better.

With a calm, I didn't know I possessed. I ran the tip of my gun up her belly, moving up between her full breasts and pointing the end at her chin. I heard her gulp. "What do you think your punishment should be, my little pet, hmmm? What do you think will fix this travesty of justice? I don't think anything can. The damage was fulfilled when he filled you with his spawn. He stole you from me and destroyed my beautiful, innocent, obedient pet." I could feel the anger pulsing through the pores of my skin. I was so angry. I didn't think I would ever find her again. Yet here we were. It was more fortune than luck that I came across her by accident. But then she just had to keep going and push my buttons.

"He has certainly provided for me better than you ever did. I am living in a magnificent house, and I feel loved. Yet, you kept me in that dark, damp basement. Naked and dirty. Threatens of rape from your men while taking me to you for a fuck to satisfy you. What sort of life was that for someone as amazing as me?" I hmphed at him. My words came out stronger than I felt inside. I raised my chin at him in defiance.

"I should fuck you one last time in that fucking ass of yours, pet. Before I destroy you. But then, where's the fun in that, hmmm? It will only be rewarding you and not punishing you, my pet. I will gain nothing from it. Such a sassy little thing these days, aren't you? Especially since you've been with my enemy." I shoved her in the back, motivating her forward. "Come on, move out into the bedroom, pet."

Oh god, he's going to rape me. I hope he doesn't hurt our baby pumpkin. It will kill me if he does. I took my time waddling out of the closet into the bedroom. I tried to delay the inevitable. Yet here I was, feeling like I was marching toward my death.

"Come on, get a hurry along, pet." I shoved the gun into her back, grinning excitedly when I made her grimace. I didn't know what my plan was going to be. I hadn't come with one. I never expected to find my pet here that he had stolen. I expected him to take her away with him. I expected the house to be empty when I got here. Especially when only a few guards were guarding his compound. I was even more surprised to see her here and pregnant. I had come here to search for my stolen USB with the backup accounts he had taken when he stole my pet. I shoved her over by the bed. "Stay there. Don't move while I decide what to do next with you, my pet."

"What do we do now, Prez?" Tomas asked when he entered the bedroom after searching their closet. "We couldn't find anything. Therefore, he must have it with him. Either that, or he has it hidden here somewhere. Maybe in a secret hidden place like a safe."

I scratched my chin. Did I do my worst to get back at that asshole Brazen? It would hurt my heart. I still had a soft spot for her. But he had ruined her for me now. I wanted to spit on this puta now that she was full of his devil spawn. Should I do my worst? Could I? What was I doing here? Should I steal her back? Bring her back home with me? Why was I thinking anything? I was killing time. She was no use to me now, I decided. It was now or never. I strode over to where she stood near the bed. "I could have given you everything, my pet. But he ruined all that for us." I immediately saw red when she interrupted me.

"You were never going to show me anything apart from that basement," she accused me.

"Now, we will never know, will we, my little pet? Hmmm..." I rubbed the end of my gun against her belly again, pissed off that she had dared to challenge me. "I should end it all now. But I won't. I will hurt you in a way you will never imagine. I will break your heart. But better still, that asshole's heart forever. I wish he were here to bear witness to what I will do next. But he will see the result of my actions.

Therefore, that will have to be enough revenge for me for now." I began running the end of my gun up and down her belly, between her breasts. I then pointed the gun at her chin. "Where do you want me to pull the trigger? Here," my gun still pointed at her chin. "Or here," moving the weapon between her breasts. "or here," pointing at her belly.

My heart froze in my chest. I was unable to breathe. I started blubbering. "Please don't hurt my baby," I begged. My heart felt like it was getting squeezed in a tight vice. My insides melted in terror of what was to come. He had given me no choice. I could see now that I would die today, along with my baby pumpkin. Brazen would come home to nothing but a bloody crime scene. My life was going to end today. I could see it now. These were going to be my last few minutes on this earth. I took my finger and pointed at my chin. I begged to god to please make it quick. I watched while he took the gun away from my chin to scratch his chin with the tip.

His eyes faced the ceiling while he contemplated his decision. I knew what I would do before I even gave her a choice. Who was I kidding? No matter what choice she made. It was always going to be the wrong one. I grabbed her hair, winding it around my hand, and pointed the gun at her belly. "No, my pet. I'm going to make you suffer. You can watch while you both die together."

I pointed the end of my gun at her belly and pulled the trigger, shooting her in the stomach. I let her slip from my fingers and fall onto the floor. I smirked while watching her scream in agony and overwhelming grief. While at the same time, watching her as she lay slowly bleeding out on the floor. I should have felt sorrow at her loss but broke out in a maniacal laugh instead. "The job is done," I said to no one in particular. This chapter was now over, even though it had never started. I walked out of the bedroom without even glancing back.

I screamed out, "Nooooo.... Help, please help me, someone," I begged. I couldn't believe he did that to me and my pumpkin. I crashed like a rock to the floor, sobbing on the floor when he let go of my hair. The pain and the grief at what he had done to me and my baby. His ultimate revenge for Brazen. I watched my blood seeping out of my belly onto the floor. I watched in disbelief while it flooded into a growing pool on the floor. I watched him leave with his men leaving me to die alone on the floor.

Omg, the pain, grief, and hopelessness I feel now. Had he killed our Pumpkin? Of course, he had, and me. Would I survive this? I didn't want to. I couldn't live without our baby. I couldn't leave my baby to be alone for eternity. I groaned in agony while watching Torres leave the room without even a backward glance. It was the last sight I was ever going to see. I wish it could be my magnificent, fantastic specimen of a man, Brazen. Instead, it was going to be of that asshole scumbag Torres.

I felt the darkness overtaking me. I felt weak with the loss of blood oozing out of my womb into a puddle on the floor. *Where are you, Brazen? Can you hear me? I love you.* I faded off into the light along with our darling little girl. *I'm so sorry that I'm leaving you behind, my love. You will be here alone to cope with our loss. I will be by your side to keep an eye on you. I'm sorry Torres found me and did this to us while you were away and unable to save us. Our little pumpkin was a girl. Now, I was in heaven together with my precious baby girl. I wouldn't leave her alone, and we would be together for eternity. We will wait for the day Daddy comes to join us in heaven. I gathered her in my arms, overcome with love for her... United in death. Mummy loves you, my baby. I'm sorry this happened to us. You never got to live and meet your daddy. We will both wait here every day and watch over your daddy forever. Until the day your daddy comes to join us. He will be with us here one day.*

Chapter Thirty Two - Brazen

I felt relieved when I saw our compound on the horizon. Thank God. I'm nearly home baby. I knew it was late, and she would probably be asleep. But I couldn't wait to jump into bed and hold her in bed. Had I known what fate awaited...

I was glad when we finally got closer to the compound. I could see the front gates come into view. Oh, fuck when we got closer, and I saw what looked like the Stoner men looking nervous and worried, loitering around the open gate. Shit, this didn't look good. Why the hell were the gates open? They should be shut. Something was wrong. "Oh god, Christa. Somethings wrong." *Fuck, it was too quiet, and my house was in darkness.*

When we got closer, my stomach dropped to the bottom of my gut, and my heart froze in my chest. My men guarding the gate were bloody and slaughtered in the driveway. I slammed my brakes on and threw my bike down at the gate entrance. No, no, no, fuck please let Christa be okay. I began running down the driveway, ignoring the Stoner leader, Big Bender, yelling at me to wait. But no, I couldn't. I had to know. If that was the front gate, what was the inside of my house like? Was Christa still safe, or had they kidnapped her?

I knew it would be bad when the front door was wide open and another bloody body was in the doorway. "Fuck! Christa," I yelled in a panic. "Where are you baby." Fuck when I smelt the strong smell of blood in the air. I was trying to swallow the lump in my throat when I saw they had trashed the house while they were at it.

"Brazen, wait!" Mo yelled from behind me.

"Where are you? Fuck" when silence was the only response I received. I ran from room to room, turning the lights on. Only to find the house wrecked in our absence. "Christa, where are you, Baby?" My deep, dark monsters began to run wild around my heart, dragging it down. Had someone taken her? God, I don't know who or what has happened to her. I began running my hands down my face in despair.

Fuck as I reached the stairs taking them two at a time in a panic. I ran towards my bedroom. "Please be asleep in bed, baby," I prayed. "That's why you can't hear me," I begged. I didn't want to fear the worst of what had happened to her in my absence. Then, I could smell the unmistakable smell of copper in the air the closer I got to our room. "Nooooo!" I yelled. I now knew what I was going to find. I finally reached the bedroom. In the distance, I could hear Mo running up the stairs and yelling.

"Brazen. Please wait for me. Don't go in there," he called out.

I couldn't wait. I had to see for myself. I turned the light on and fell to my knees with the sight before. I was running my fingers through my hair; I couldn't believe the picture before my eyes. My whole life was gone before my eyes. Panic overwhelmed, making it hard to breathe. "Oh god no, why did they have to her and our baby?" Hot tears streamed down my face when the dam burst.

I summoned the strength to crawl across the floor to her lifeless, bloody body. I thumped my chest in despair and anger at who did this to her and me for going away and leaving her. I pulled my wife onto my lap, feeling for a pulse, but there was none. "No," I wailed, cradling my dead wife on my lap, glancing up at the ceiling as if I would find my answers up there while cursing God for allowing this to happen.

Mo appeared in the doorway. "Jesus fucking Christ. Motherfuckers. I'm so sorry, Brazen." Even his voice shook with sorrow.

I watched a trail of silvery tears fall from Mo's eyes and down his face. I know all my men loved her very much. She was the sort of person whom everyone she met loved her. I sobbed into her hair, both gone. I didn't know how I was ever going to survive this. My heart stilled and then died in my chest before I felt my heart shrinking to the size of a walnut. I was shattered beyond belief at the scene before me. I knew there was no coming back from this. My heart no longer wanted to be in this world either, with the love of my life gone.

"Fuck I'm so sorry, brother," Mo tried to console me while he stood over me, sorrow written across his face.

"Thanks, Mo, though it will never bring them back."

"I know. We'll search for the security footage. We'll find those fuckers who did this. We're going to make them pay. I promise you, Brazen."

"I'm going to be the one to kill the fucker too. I'm going to make him suffer and pay for what he did. Even if it's the last thing I do in this life."

"Hey, brother, no talking like that! I know you're suffering right now... It would be best if you pull yourself together soon. Your grief is still raw, and we'll get this fucker and make him pay. How do you want to handle this? Do I call the cops, or do you want to do this our way?"

"God, I don't know, Mo. Whatever you think is best." I ran my fingers through my hair and pulled it at the ends, wanting to pull it out in grief and frustration. I needed to get someone to pay.

"There is a way, brother," he muttered, sounding hopeful. "We can do it our way and give them a proper burial and hold a funeral and burial on the property here. Think about it and let me know. Don't take too long. I'll leave you alone to grieve while I make some arrangements."

"I want to do it our way. But I want to do it the other way and give them a proper burial, and then I have somewhere to grieve. Plus, I would like to know what our baby was since we were leaving it as a surprise for when the baby was born." *Please forgive me, baby. I hope you can hear me up there. I hope you didn't suffer. If I knew this was coming, I would never have left you here alone. I would have stayed to protect you. I'll find out who this was and make them pay. I want you to know I am so sorry. I know I can never make up to you. But I wish I could.*

I watched Mo leave. Once he left the room, I put my arms around her, pulling up against my chest. I buried my nose in her hair, holding her tight in my arms one last time. I was becoming a blubbery mess. I know I was contaminating the crime scene, but I didn't give a fuck. Once I got the tears out of my system. I tried to pull myself together. I knew I needed to go to Mo and help him with arrangements. But I didn't want to leave her here alone. She had been all alone in her final moments. I stood up. I bent down, picking her up. I placed her on our bed and covered her with the quilt cover. I kissed her forehead and left the room in search of Mo. I didn't want to leave her again. But we needed to find out who did this.

Chapter Thirty Three - Brazen

After searching the house, I finally found Mo in the security room. Busy checking the security footage. "Any luck yet?" I dropped down like a lead weight with all the grief of the world on my shoulders in the chair next to him.

"Not yet, but I've only started watching the tapes."

I sat next to him, watching while he scrolled through the footage taken while we were gone. I wanted to see the fucker who dared to come on my property and do this to my wife and child. He or they were going to pay. I sucked in a breath when I saw who it was. "Torres," I growled. "What the fuck did he come here for? We haven't seen or heard anything from him for ages. He got enraged that I took his girls. Then nothing. I thought he got over it. I note that he has maybe been stewing over this for a while, it seems. Now, he's finally returned for revenge. God, it's all my fault they're gone."

"Hey," Mo said. "Don't beat yourself up over this. It's not your fault. He was here looking for something, I reckon. Otherwise, why was he here trashing the place? What was he searching for? Probably that fucking drive that he thinks we stole. Sure, he probably knows that we took those women. But we didn't take anything else, only them. I don't know why he thinks we have that drive of his. He was never on our radar. It's been a few years now. Why now? He struck it lucky for him but unluckily for Christa being alone. Christa was here alone in her own house. You left security for her. It's not like you left her alone by herself. He came prepared for everyone, which left the men here outnumbered. Christa was an innocent victim here."

"Yeah! You're right. I wish I had taken her with us now. I thought she would be safer here at home. I wasn't expecting any trouble, especially from him. I still don't know what he was here for. But he better make sure he watches his back. He's a dead man walking now."

"Now hear me, Brazen. I want you to promise me that you won't go and do anything stupid and go alone without backup. We've got your back, brother." Mo was insistent. "You'll be a dead man walking if you go in there alone."

"Who cares! My life that had any meaning has gone," I sniffed. Then, I got up to search for a bottle of bourbon.

"Hey, brother, we do care. We're family, too. I know you're hurting. We are, too. She was your everything. All your men, me included here, cared for her too. We hate that she's gone too. I left some men down there in tears at her loss. But you're still here, and we all care about what happens to you. You hear me."

"Yeah," while flipping him the bird when I got up to leave Mo to it.

"Where are you going now?"

"To get me a drink, not that it's any of your business. You got something to say about that brother?"

"I could. But I'm not going to say it. I'll have one while you're at it. Never trust the man that drinks alone."

I went to the drink cabinet, opened it, and pulled out a bottle and a glass. I returned to the security room. I sat back in the chair, poured a drink, and shoved the glass toward Mo. I leaned back in the chair and took a large swig from the bottle. I raised my eyebrow when I saw Mo gaze a critical eye over me. "You got something to say? Spit it out. I'm waiting."

"Nothing! Mo sighed in defeat. It's one drink, even when it's the whole bottle. You have your drink while I finish mine," I leaned back in the chair, crossing my right leg over my left knee. I sighed and raised my glass, toasting. "Here's to you, Christa. We'll miss you around here, babe. We're sorry for leaving you here without enough security."

"Yeah, what you say?" I raised my bottle in the air and spilled a few drops over my jeans. I was so clumsy. I needed this whole bottle to shut out what had happened to my family. "I don't know how I will survive without her, Mo." I let forth a fresh burst of tears burst. Now they had finished pricking my eyes. I leaned forward, resting my elbows on my knees. I held a tight grip on the bottle for some support. I watched my tears drip down my cheeks. They fell onto the floor, and I watched them leave an ever-increasing puddle. Finally, I sobbed, "Will you ever forgive me, baby? I know I'll never forgive myself. Rest in peace, my sweet angels. We'll kill that bastard to revenge your taking from us."

"I've got your back, Brazen." I tried reassuring him and patting him on the back, but I'm not sure it helped much. "We'll get that bastard for what he did. I promise you, Brazen."

"Thanks," I stuttered through my tears. "What's going to happen now?"

"We'll do whatever you decide. If you make to make it official, we can report it. Or we can do it our way and give them a decent burial out here on the property."

"I want to make it official and determine whether our baby is a boy or a girl. But then I don't want all the cops coming here taking over and putting up with all their bullshit and questions."

"You better decide soon, Brother, cos we can't leave her there much longer if you're going the official route. I have an old school friend who's a D' named Penrod. I can contact him to get some diplomacy on the matter and keep it out of the media."

I put the bottle on the desk, scrubbing my hands down my face. *I always thought I would go first due to my line of work. Never in my wildest dreams did I imagine that she would go before me.* "God, why her and not me," I begged. I grimaced when I caught Mo out the corner of my eye, turning and giving me that stink-eye look. "I guess go the official route but not show them our security footage. I want her treated with respect and given a proper burial. It would be nice to know what the sex of our baby was. I can then include our pumpkin with their name on the gravestone."

"On it! I'll make the call to Penrod," Mo insisted.

I waved the bottle at him before taking my next swig. "I should. I'm the Prez, and it's my house."

"Yeah, but I'm your second in command and know the detective. You're currently not in any fit state to do this." I picked up my cell and dialed the local police department, asking for Detective Penrod. "Hi Penrod, it's me, Mo from the old days at college. I need to report a home invasion and a murder. But I need it kept on the down low and don't need it getting out in the media if we can help it. Thanks. I appreciate anything you can do to help us." I gave him all the required details, and he assured me that help was coming. I stood up when I finished the call. "Come on, Brazen, it's time to get up and get out of here. They're on their way. We need to meet them when they arrive, preferably with you still sober. I need to lock this room behind us."

"I know! I only want to hide away and drown my sorrows. But I must do the right thing by them and make sure they treat my babies respectfully. I intend to give them the burial and send off they both deserve." I followed Mo out, watching while he locked the door behind us. I was at a loss for what to do next. Luckily, I had Mo, who directed me to follow him to the lounge room to wait. Along the way, I asked Mo, "what if they ask if we have any security footage of what happened? They're not fools and will see all our cameras around here."

We'll worry about that when it happens. I'll see if I can get away with a little white lie of them wiping the footage of what happened from the hard drive. I've already saved it and sent it to my laptop cloud. Then I deleted the recording from the hard drive it's usually saved to. I'll watch it later to see who and what happened."

Chapter Thirty Four - Brazen

When the cops finally arrived, I couldn't face them. I left it up to Mo to tell our story. I couldn't handle the situation. The cops asked too many questions I didn't want to answer. I have never felt so helpless in all my life. I didn't know how I would survive without the love of my life here anymore. I wish it had been me. I'll never live with myself again now that I've lost them.

I watched with anger while they walked around surveying the upturned furniture. They searched through drawers that had been emptied and their contents tossed all around the room that they had been in. How dare they. I knew they were doing their job, but it still hurt. I should have left it to us to deal with. But I couldn't. I needed to know the sex of my baby now that I would never meet them.

They eventually got to my bedroom, which they had left until last. They were demanding us to tell them who did this. We must have some idea. Fortunately, Mo convinced them that we didn't know who had come here and murdered my wife. He had to explain that my DNA might be on her body as I lifted her body off the floor and lay her on the bed.

Then, the way the cops carried on made it sound like we had done this ourselves, and I had murdered my wife. I should have known this would be a huge mistake calling the police. I should have left it up to us to deal with it and bury her here on our property. Hindsight is always accessible on reflection. I guess Mo's cop friend being here helped relieve the tension somewhat. In the middle of all this confrontation, the coroner came to assess the scene and deliberate on the cause of Christa's death. Which, of course, was determined to be a gunshot. Which I already knew. She decided that it was from a .22 revolver.

I moved into another room when I knew they would bring her body out for transport to the coroner's office for an autopsy. I couldn't watch when she left her home for the last time. It broke my heart. I didn't even know how I would live here without her. It was noisy now with all the cops and the forensics team going through everything. But soon, they would all be gone, and it would be too quiet. If I could ever sleep again, I would have to move into another bedroom.

No way could I go in that room ever again. It was our room and not my room. Too many precious memories were now spoilt by the sight I never expected to see. After what happened in our room, all I would ever see again was her bloody body lying on the floor in a pool of blood. I would lock the door and never enter it again. I would also have to close the nursery door. I couldn't bear to walk past and glance in any longer.

I would see everything we had already done in preparation for the arrival of our baby. I loved the few extras that Christa had added while I was away. But it tore at my heart. Now, our baby would never see the room we had decorated with our special love. Christa would now be up there in heaven caring for our baby. Thank God they wouldn't be alone. They could be together. I wish I could be with them. Now, I was out to avenge their deaths. Torres better watch out. He better watch his back and sleep with one eye open. I was coming for him.

I was glad when everyone left; the house was mine once again. Only Mo, myself, and the rest of our men. Everyone was now out on extra duty and on high alert for any more trouble from Torres. Though I didn't expect him to return, he had done what he came for. Torres had come into my home, ripped my heart out, and thrown it away. I didn't want it any longer anyway after this. I'd had enough; I was exhausted. I decided to go to bed, though whether I got any sleep was another matter.

I took my bottle of bourbon upstairs with me, taking another swig on my way to the spare bedroom. I had called Valeria in to make the bed up for me. I told her I'd pay her a bonus for coming in, especially for me and the extra work I had asked her to do for me over the next few days. Then, I told her to leave my bedroom alone. I would get our clean-up guys in to fix that mess up in that room. Along with cleaning up the mess Torres and his men had made around the house.

She made some food for us to eat. But I couldn't stomach any food. I started feeling tipsy now with a wobbly boot, staggering along the hallway to my new room. I puffed out a breath of air. God, how was I going to sleep alone now? I was used to my gorgeous wife beside me. I hiccoughed a sob, and the tears flowed down my face. I put my back against the wall and slid down. I raised my knees and put my arms around them. I rested my forehead on my knees while my jeans soaked up my tears. I must have fallen asleep in this position. Next, I was aware of Mo shaking my shoulder, trying to wake me up. "Go away, leave me the fuck alone," I cursed at him.

"Nope, not happening. You can't sleep here. It would be best if you get in a bed." I grabbed him by the elbow, helping Brazen up. With a bit of effort due to his dead drunken weight, I managed to get him up from the floor. I put his arm around my neck and helped him onto the bed. "I know you're hurting, but you can't do this to yourself, Braze. It would be best if you were there to get through the funeral. You can't miss that, or you will never forgive yourself."

"I know, Mo. But it hurts so bad. I feel like I've been stabbed in the heart, and the knife is still twisting around. How do I get through this?"

"Yeah, I'll be honest, it's going to be hard when someone you think will be your forever is suddenly not here anymore. I can't deny you that. You will keep blaming yourself for the rest of your life. I know it's easy to say now because it's not me in your position." I gave him a bro slap across the shoulder. "We're here for you and support you. It's different from having your babies here with you. But we'll get that fucker to pay for what he did to your family. I promise. Even if it takes until my dying day, I won't let it rest."

Chapter Thirty Five - Brazen

I woke up not sure how much sleep I got. I went downstairs and grabbed another bourbon bottle to return to my room. I walked into the spare room, trying not to stare at the closed door to my old bedroom as I walked past. I stormed past as if something in there would get me. I walked into the spare room, now my bedroom, and slammed the door shut behind me. My heart was broken as the sound echoed around the space. The only furniture in the room was the bed and an armoire. This house was now an empty shell of what it once was. There was no life left in this house anymore. My beloved wife had been stolen from me. My heart was lifeless, like an enormous vacant rock in my chest. What will my life be like now without you, my sweet baby? Damn, why did I have to go there? I felt the well overflowing again, and the tears washed down my face.

Fuck it; I forgot to bring my bourbon bottle with me. I turned and opened the door, yelling out, "Mo. Bring me my bottle of bourbon, will you."

"I don't think you need it, Buddy. Drinking isn't going to solve anything, you know."

"Yeah, I do. But it will help kill the pain I'm feeling. You better watch out if I need to come down and get it. Shut up. I heard that sigh." I heard him coming up the stairs *about fucking time.* When he stood in front of me, casting me a look of pity. I snatched the bottle from his hand, "thanks." I returned inside the bedroom, slamming the door shut in his face. I know he didn't deserve that. But I needed to be alone, and I didn't need any lectures from him.

I took another swig out of the bottle before collapsing on the bed. How was I ever going to sleep without her next to me anymore? Fuck I couldn't even go back into the bedroom yet. Cursing now, I had to get up and turn the fucking light off. I staggered across the room, turned it off, and felt my way back again since I wasn't used to being in this room.

I lay there alone in the cold, hard bed in the dark. I wished you were here lying next to me, baby. I can't sleep without you here with me anymore. I hope you can hear me wherever you are in heaven. I need you now like I never have before. I'm so sorry I wasn't here for you. I wish that I had taken you with me when we left. Hindsight is always favorable, but now it was too late.

Fuck it; I can't sleep. I was lying here in the dark, hugging my bottle and, at the same time, glancing up at the ceiling, seeing nothing but darkness. It was all I deserved for going away and leaving my poor, defenseless wife and baby at home alone. I kept seeing the bloody scene in my bedroom every time I closed my eyes. I sat up, took another dose of medicine from my bottle, and swung my legs over the edge of the bed. I stood up after a couple of minutes. I need to get her pillow and hug it to see if I can sleep smelling her scent. I will never wash her pillow ever again. I staggered up and flung the door open, hearing it crash against the wall. I used the wall for support as I walked to my bedroom. I took a massive gulp before I put my hand on the doorknob. "You can do this," I mutter, resting my forehead against the door. It took me a few minutes to gather the courage to open the door.

It still hadn't been appropriately cleaned, leaving a hint of blood in the air, making me want to vomit. But I held it together, swallowing down the bile threatening to rear its ugly head. I flicked the light on, blinded by the brightness. I shut my eyes, waiting a few seconds before trying again. I tried not to stare at the spot where her body had been left. But my eyes were drawn to the location, and I could not help myself. Fortunately, the blood had been cleaned up, but it still left a stain on the wood, with the smell lingering in the air. I went around my side of the bed, reaching across to snare her pillow. I pulled it close to my face and sniffed her pillow. I could still smell the light scent of her perfume there. I wanted to cry but couldn't do it on her pillow. It would make her scent disappear. I convinced myself. I'm so lost without you, baby. I'm sorry, Baby. Even though you're not here with me, you'll forgive me one day. I know I'll never forgive myself. I need to get out of here. It's too depressing. I took her pillow with me and returned to the spare room.

I returned to the spare room and lay back on the bed, lying on my side and hugging her pillow close to my chest. I took in a large sniff. It felt fainter, but there was still a slight lingering smell of her scent. I turned on my back, bringing her pillow with me. I grabbed the bottle off the bedside table, sat up, and took another swig. Fuck, it was empty. I flung it across the room, where it hit the wall and smashed, the pieces falling and tinkling to the floor. I lay back on the pillow, clutching your pillow to me as if my life depended on it. It did. I eventually fell asleep dreaming of the memories of our sweet time together.

Chapter Thirty Six - Brazen

I don't know how I made it through the next few days. I suppose if it hadn't been for Mo being along with me every step of the way. He was always there hovering and there if I needed him for decisions I didn't know to make. I knew what the autopsy results would be. It was obvious without needing an autopsy. She died from a single gunshot, a bullet to her stomach. I found out our little pumpkin was a girl. I cried for the life that she would never live. All thanks to me, her father. I called her Delilah Rose. I like to think Christa would have loved Pumpkin's name too. Delilah was on our list of names if it was a girl, and I thought Rose was a lovely name for her middle name. They seemed to go together.

All too soon, it was the day of the funeral. I don't know how I would get through this day, let alone the funeral. I struggled to put my suit on and hold back the tears threatening to break loose. I finally got there dressed and slung my jacket over the bed to put on later when it was time to go. I then had a shot of bourbon, then another. It didn't kill the pain but helped numb the pain. I didn't want this day ever to come. I didn't want to say goodbye to the love of my life as it was the final fond farewell. One that I never wanted, and it was all my fault. Mo came in to see if I was ready. He brought my anger to a head when he took my life support away from me.

"You don't need any more of this, Buddy. You don't want to show yourself up being drunk at their funeral. I know you're hurting badly, but this doesn't fix it. I know..."

"Yeah, I know you're right. I want the pain to go away. Will it ever go away?"

"It never really goes away, Braze. It's always there simmering in some form. Enough that you never forget them," he sighed forlornly.

"You never told me whom you lost, Mo. Was it a wife or girlfriend?"

I slapped Brazen on the shoulder. "One day. But today is not that day. Okay."

"Yeah, I'm sorry for whatever loss you suffered, Mo. I know how painful it can be now. But when you lose the one you thought was forever in your life before their time."

"Thanks, pal," Mo muttered. "Now come on, the limo is here to take us."

I shrugged my jacket, following Mo down the stairs to the waiting limo. All the other guys and family members that could fit were already inside, waiting solemnly for us. I got in last after Mo and slammed the door shut. I leaned forward, staring at the floor, wringing my hands together in sorrow. It was made all the worse by no one talking to everyone else, sitting in grief, and feeling my pain.

Christa was the most excellent, fantastic woman to ever walk in this world, and she always had a smile and a kind word for everyone. They didn't have their heart ripped out like me, leaving a jagged hole in their chest as I did. My beautiful wife but my baby girl who never got to live. I'll never forgive myself for what happened to them both. Though at least I gave Christa a chance to live and be happy with me. Which is something she would never have if Torres still had her. I could try to convince myself of that.

It was the longest ride of my life, but we eventually arrived at the funeral home where the service would be held. I had chosen a lovely funeral celebrant, lady Gail, to do our service. Mo would get up on my behalf and do a memorial I had written for Christa. I didn't think I could talk and see everyone's faces. I would crumble and break apart in front of everyone. I know I'm a piece of chickenshit and should man up. But I didn't know how in a situation like this. I had never been here before. It was one of my own family, not a friend or acquaintance. We all piled out, and I stared at the hearse, its rear door raised. Ready for us to take her from her ride and begin the long walk down the aisle for her service. I choked up, not prepared but knowing I had to do this in honor of my two babies.

We raised the coffin to our shoulders and began the trek down the aisle towards the front of the room to place my two babies for their final swan song. I don't know how I made it. My legs shook badly while I walked down the aisle in the middle, and everyone observed us while we filed past. Some wiped a tear away, and others broke out into a sob as we passed, making me want to break down and fall to my knees in my grief, feeling their sorrow. We placed her coffin gently down on the catafalque. I took the photo off the easel and placed it on their coffin. I bent down and kissed her coffin, wishing I could give her one final kiss, but I wanted a closed casket service. The cold, polished wood casket felt hard beneath my lips; there was nothing like kissing her soft lips. I patted the coffin and went to take my seat in the front row next to Mo.

My eyes were drawn to the coffin entombing my wife and baby. I glanced longingly over at the magnificent photo of my wife in a happier time atop their coffin. I felt like a knife had stabbed my heart. It broke my heart because I had none of my poor baby who never got to live. She was taken before she even got to take a breath in this world. The waterworks finally broke and let loose, running like a stream down my face. I glanced over at Mo and gave him a weak grin when he patted me on the shoulder, giving me some strength. I sucked in a breath, wiped the tears from my face, and sat stoically as the celebrant spoke of my wife's life like it was a dream, and they knew her personally.

Before too long, it was Mo's turn to get up and do my memorial speech on my behalf. I had prepared to tell everyone about our short but sweet and happy life together. Before, she was brutally taken away from me. Even Mo was breaking up, only pausing when his voice shook with emotion and tears ran down his cheeks. I watched as he brushed them angrily away; I'm sure he was lost in his memories of the beautiful memories that we had all once had.

Finally, he had to compose himself before continuing the prepared memorial talk. Once he had finished, he cleared his throat, telling people he would like to tell everyone what a stunning, fantastic woman Christa was and how she was my rock. She got into everyone's hearts, and they would do anything to protect her. She was always there to cover and care for them. There was a huge empty hole in everyone's hearts and lives with her loss of life. He cleared his throat and gave a curt nod to everyone, then left the podium to go and sit back to Brazen. I don't think a dry eye was left in the place after I recollected her life with our family.

A few more friends got up to speak of their recollections of life with Christa. She made a significant impact on many lives, more than I realized. Once, everyone who wished to say something had their turn. Mo got up to tell everyone to return to the club after for a feed and reminisce more about Christa and her life. It brought a giant lump to my throat, making it hard to swallow and causing more tears. This was finally it. Now, it was real. I knew she was gone and would never hear her call out for me.

Even though it had been a couple of weeks since it all happened, I could still imagine she would walk back through the door. Or come searching for me in the house, but seeing the coffin before I brought finality to it all. Me, Mo, and the other pallbearers stood up. I grabbed a rose and sauntered to the casket to say goodbye to my two babies. I kissed the fingers on my right hand and placed them on the coffin, giving them a last kiss. I whispered, "sleep, my babies. Sleep peacefully until I join you one day. Then we will all be together again. I stood aside to let the other mourners say their final farewells. It was all I could do to stop myself from throwing the coffin lid open. I wanted to hug her and never wanted to let go. I didn't want to say goodbye. I wanted to be with her.

Once the last of the mourners had said their final farewells. Mo, me, and the other pallbearers assembled, ready to take them on their final journey and prepared to take Christa and our sweet baby Delilah down the aisle on their journey to their final resting place. It was the most challenging walk I had ever made for the second time today.

I was reluctant to put them back in the hearse. I wanted to open it and take them out, hugging them one last time. I was losing my mind with my grief, it seems. I held my breath and gave their coffin one last touch with my hand. I felt sick with grief and what they had been through. My lifestyle had ruined their lives. I then made a vow to them that I would hunt down Torres, make him suffer, and pay for their deaths.

Chapter Thirty Seven - Brazen

I don't know how I did it. But I managed to survive the rest of the afternoon in a house full of noise with everyone chattering around me. I began to feel claustrophobic. It felt like the room was closing in around me. My thoughts overwhelmed me with the place that had once been my haven. Now, it had become my living hell. I felt like I couldn't live in this house anymore. There were too many memories here now. I stood watching everyone appearing happy and laughing. While at the same time, I felt broken inside. While I stood alone leaning against the wall, drinking my bourbon. I was trying to keep out of Mo's way, hoping he wouldn't notice I was only drinking and wasn't eating anything.

Occasionally, someone would approach me and offer their condolences. I'd try at least to show some concern and nod, offering my thanks for their sympathy. Eventually, Mo must have seen me standing here with a glass in my hand, not moving. I grimaced when I saw him heading in my direction. Ready to argue with him over what he had to say. No doubt I wouldn't like what he had to say. I waited for him to speak first.

"What are you doing over here, Braze? I see you nursing that glass of whisky. Don't think I haven't noticed you're here drinking and not eating."

"Yeah, it doesn't pay to think you wouldn't notice," I gritted.

"Yes! I notice everything that goes on around here. It's my job," he said compassionately. "I know it's hard, Braze. It's never easy losing the love of your life. But drinking doesn't help. Trust me, I know."

I turned to stare at him. You going to tell me the story then?"

"Nope! Not today. One day, but today is not the day." He leaned against the wall with his hands behind his back, observing the people still left. "Do you want me to get rid of everyone now? Give yourself a break and a rest. I'm sure you need it since it's been a long, sad day."

Still bitter and twisted over everything that had happened, I now had to put up with the wake on top of everything else. I gritted out, "please, do. I want everyone out of here now. I want to be here by myself." I was pissed that people still needed to be here eating and drinking.

Mo pushed himself away from the wall, ready to chase everyone out of the house if needed. He wolf-whistled to catch everyone's attention. Once, everyone was finally silent and listening to what he was about to say. "On behalf of Brazen, I'd like to thank everyone for coming along to remember our memories of Christa and for baby Delilah Rose, who sadly never got to take a breath in this life. I want to ask you all to take your leave so Brazen can take some time to grieve his loss in private." He leaned back against the wall after saying his piece and nodding to everyone as they all murmured around the room.

People came over to give him their condolences one last time and slapped him on the shoulder on their way out the door. Brazen lifted his chin and nodded as they passed, unable to say anything in return. I knew I would break if I did, and I didn't want to do that in front of everyone. I have a reputation to uphold. Therefore, I didn't want to show weakness, although my one flaw had already been discovered and disposed of.

Once, silence reigned again in the house except for those who stayed there. I took my leave and went up to the bedroom. I went to my armoire and grabbed the whiskey bottle hidden under some underwear. I breathed a sigh of relief. It was still there. Mo hadn't found it and had taken it away from me. I went over and collapsed on the bed and took a swig, grimacing when it burnt on the way down. I sighed, hating how the sound echoed in the empty room. I knew it was doing him no favor drinking like this. But it helped ease the ache in my chest while I rubbed my fist across his chest where his heart lay below—now shattered in a million pieces that could never be fixed again. In my gut, I wanted revenge and would hunt Torres down and ensure he paid for ruining my life and Christa's.

I sat there wallowing in my self-pity until I had nearly finished the bottle of whisky. Despite that, my heart still ached in my chest. No matter how much I keep rubbing that spot in my chest. I carefully put the bottle on the bedside table without knocking it over. I eventually collapsed back on the bed in a drunken stupor, and soon, loud snores echoed around the bedroom.

Chapter Thirty Eight – Brazen

I awoke the following day groaning when Mo entered my bedroom, ripping the curtains open and letting the sun's full effect on the room.

"Fuck off, Mo. Please leave me alone." Even saying that made my headache and the pounding in my head worse. I was so hungover. "Oh god," I grumbled at his rude intrusion into my nightmares. I rubbed my hands across my face, scratching them on my stubble.

"He won't help you either," Mo mumbled. "Here, I've brought you some coffee. Get that in you. Have a shower. You smell like a distillery, and then come down and have something to eat."

"Who are you, my mother or something?" I growled at Mo, glaring at him.

"Nope, and I don't pretend to be. I'm your best friend who cares for you. Pull yourself together, Braze, be a leader, and come downstairs to see your men."

"Whatever." I rolled over and tried sitting up and felt dizziness come over me, and bile started to rise in my stomach. "Fuck why do I do this to myself" I groaned.

"I tried to warn you, but you brought it all on yourself. Therefore, I have no sympathy for you." I roughly grabbed Brazen under the arms and dragged him to a sitting position against the headboard. I grabbed the cup of coffee I had out on the bedside table. "Here, now, drink that first. Before you attempt to do anything else, for fucks sake."

"I'm sorry, Mo, for being such as ass," I apologized.

"Apology accepted. You are in mourning. Therefore, I'll let you off this time. But now I need you to pull yourself together and return to work. We can't let others in and take over on our lot while you're full of self-pity."

"I know! Sorry, I lost the plot wallowing in my self-pity. I was once a strong man, but this broke me. I should be here plotting and planning revenge for their deaths."

"I know. It is hard, but now you're talking. That's my Braze coming back," he grinned.

I took a sip of the hot coffee, needing to feel the pain of the hot drink burning down to my stomach. It wouldn't be enough to sober me up, but it would help. Then watch out, Torres, you'll pay for what you did to my family. I decided there, and then I would take my revenge solo. I wasn't going to tell Mo or anyone else my plans. It was going to be between Torres and me. He was mine and mine alone. Mo would hate it, but I didn't care. It was my family that was gone, not his.

"Right! I'll leave you now and go down to grab myself some breakfast. I expect to see you shortly when you've had your shower." Mo left the room, shutting the door behind him.

Thank fuck for that. I finished my coffee, pulled my weary hungover ass off the bed, and headed to the bathroom for my shower. I turned the shower on full blast as hot as I could stand. I shed my clothes and got under the water, leaning my head against the wall. It was great feeling the water hit my head and run over my body, watching it go down the plug hole. Once, I felt able to stand without falling over. I grabbed the shampoo and washed my hair. Once that was done, I washed my body with the body wash. I began scrubbing my body, trying to hurt and feel something other than the hurt in my heart and the pounding in my head.

Once the water started getting cold, I decided it was time to get out. I grabbed the towel, dried myself off, tied the towel around my waist, and entered the bedroom. I went over to my armoire, grabbed jeans and a shirt, and dressed. I took a deep breath. It was now time to go downstairs and face the music. It would be a long day with this hangover, but at least the shower helped.

When I arrived in the kitchen, the table was filled with chatter. Everyone was suddenly silent when I entered the room. I nodded. "Don't stop on my account. Carry on…" I waved them on while I headed to the counter to grab a couple of aspirin and a mug of coffee to deal with this hangover. When my back was turned, everyone went back to their conversations.

It didn't worry me; I only wanted to be left alone. I kept trying to kid myself that was the case, but what did I know? Ugh, I could feel the bile rise and hit my throat with the smell of bacon cooking. I didn't want anything to eat, but maybe I should. Otherwise, I might start drinking again instead of planning my revenge on Torres with the other men.

I was angry at them when I had no right to be. But none of them knows what it feels like to lose their forever home. It always felt like I was coming home when I saw her. Now, she's not here anymore; it doesn't feel like my home anymore. She wasn't here to fill it with her presence and personality.

I grabbed a piece of bacon from the pan and nibbled on it on my way to sit at the table with the others. I sat there listening but offered nothing to add to the ongoing conservations. My mind was in other places, plotting and planning in my head, oblivious to everything around me.

"Earth to Braze," said Mo, waving his hand in my face.

"Sorry, I was miles away," I apologized. "Getting lost in my mind."

"Well, don't get too lost in there, pal. We still need you. Are you okay? It's okay not to be okay. You know that. You are especially considering what's happened in your life and ours. She was a beautiful woman and didn't deserve what happened to her. We will get him, I promise."

"He's mine when we get him. No one else but me will end him."

"Sure, Braze, we have your back. When we get him, he's all yours. I've got my feelers out to see where he's hiding."

"When you know, let me know," I gritted out. "I want him to suffer while he pays for what he did."

Chapter Thirty Nine – Brazen & Mo
Brazen

I had a restless sleep, and even a few swigs of whisky out of the bottle didn't help. I tossed and turned. The more I thought about what had happened to Christa, the angrier I got at Torres. No one had been able to find him. But I was determined to seek my revenge on my family come hell or high water. He was mine. I groaned, rubbing my hands across my face. Sleep wasn't happening, so I got up and sat on the edge of the bed, running my hands across my face. How can everyone else live their life? All going on as usual, as if nothing had ever happened here? I sat there wallowing in my grief and misery. Yeah, I know another pity party, for one.

I glanced over at the clock. It was 5 a.m. I may as well get up. Sleep wasn't happening. I grabbed my jeans off the floor and put them on. I grabbed a T-shirt and some socks out of my armoire. I put the T-shirt on and then sat on the bed to put on my socks and boots. I went downstairs to grab a coffee and have a smoke. I strolled down the stairs, and silence reigned in the house. Everyone must still be asleep. Brilliant, it meant that I wouldn't have to connect with anyone.

I put some coffee on to brew while I waited. I leaned against the countertop. When it was ready, I poured myself a cup, walked out to the patio, and lit a smoke. I looked out over the backyard, feeling like a dot in the matrix. It made me feel small standing here. I blew smoke rings in the air, watched them fade, and sipped my coffee. It didn't feel like home anymore without the love, laughter, and chatter from Christa. She was always excited about buying things for our baby and showing them to me at the end of the day in our alone time.

It made me smile, although it was a bittersweet memory of what could have been.

I was angry that Torres was still walking somewhere like nothing had happened. My life was now over. Now, the two most important people in my life were gone. I downed the rest of my coffee in one gulp and ground my cigarette in the ashtray on the table. I needed to go for a ride. Freedom might help clear my mind. I went inside and grabbed my keys off the rack hanging on the wall. I walked out the front door, closing it quietly behind me, trying not to wake anyone. I entered the garage and rolled my bike outside. Once outside, I hit the ignition and roared off down the driveway. The darkness slowly faded while the sun began to rise on the horizon.

****

Mo

Fuck what was that? I swear I heard a bike roar into life in the driveway. Shit, it is a bike as I scrambled out of bed, getting caught up in the sheets in my haste. "Fuck" while I tried to untangle my feet before I face-planted on the floor. I bet it's Braze going out on a fucking death wish mission. I fucking told him not to go by himself and to take backup when he decided when the time was right. I have no idea where he's going either since we've had no intel on where Torres is basing himself. Not that I was aware of unless that asshole did and didn't share it with me or the others.

I grabbed my jeans and put them on, followed by my T-shirt and boots. I ran down the hallway, banging on doors as I went. "Wake up! We need to go after Brazen. He's going to hell. We need to save him. Emergency church meeting downstairs now." I could hear men groaning on the other side of their doors with the rude intrusion into their peaceful sleep. I grabbed my jacket and sat at the table, hoping they didn't take too long to get there. I knew we didn't have time for that, but we needed to collect and gather our thoughts together before we left. I paced the floor, then went over to the stairway, yelling. "Hurry up, men, this is a life-or-death emergency."

Glad when it must've dawned on them, I could hear footsteps rushing across the floors of their bedrooms, followed by them hurriedly getting dressed. Relief came when they came running down the stairs.

I was receiving bewildering stares from the men asking me, "What the emergency was?" Or the other scenario, "Where was the fire?"

"It's Brazen. He's gone out on his bike to god knows where. I'm afraid he's gone after Torres. We have no intel on where he is hiding out."

"Fuck" was the response, followed by chatter amongst themselves on their theories.

I let out a loud whistle. "Quiet everyone. We need to come up with a plan five minutes ago. He will be outnumbered wherever he's gone in search of Torres. We'll try the last place we went to see if he is holed up. Where did we rescue the women from? If we have no luck there, we'll have to regroup and find other places to search for him and his men."

Anthony asked, "how do you know he hasn't only gone out for an early morning ride?"

"With his current mind over losing his family and his need for revenge. He's been my friend for years, and I know how his mind works. I know I would be doing the same if it were me. However, I would take back up, not go alone."

"Fair enough," Anthony replied to me, nodding. "Well, let us get suited up and prepare to be ready for revenge if we find him."

"If? When do I think you mean? Hurry up, everyone; time is of the essence. Let's meet out the front after we get our weapons." I rushed with everyone to get my keys and gun out of the cabinet before heading to my bike. I started it while waiting for everyone else to assemble. Once we were all assembled, it was time to go. I waved my finger in the air for everyone to follow me, and we headed down the driveway with our roar filling the air and breaking the silence of the cool, calm morning. No doubt it wouldn't end this way of that, I was sure.

Chapter Forty - Brazen

I could feel the wind whistling through my hair while I sped down the freeway, searching for Torres. Revenge was mine. He would finally get to pay for what he did to my family. I had heard he was back at his old place where I had found the love of my life and the other women. I probably had a death wish coming on my own. But it was mine to give, and he needed to pay.

I could recall the last time I said goodbye to her. Little did I know it would be for the very last time. I kissed her and tasted her one last time, plunging my tongue deep into her mouth, unable to get enough of her sweet cinnamon taste. I also felt my baby's bump poking my stomach one last time. She was getting full of our baby growing within her body. I smiled with pride when her pregnant tummy ground into me while I passionately kissed her, not wanting to leave her, but I had no choice.

I was getting close, and anger was brewing in my belly while I bit my lip, almost tasting the revenge in my mouth. Destiny was mine. I would make the coward pay for the death of my woman and my poor, defenseless baby. I didn't care how much noise I made when I neared the compound. I rolled to a halt outside the gate, turned my bike off, and got off my bike. I walked over to the compound's entrance like I owned the place. I was stunned to see that all was quiet. Not even a soul was there guarding the gate. Maybe it was a trap. Perhaps he knew I was coming.

I couldn't believe my luck. The gate was shut, but someone had forgotten to lock the padlock. Fate or God was on my side. Someone must have been in a hurry. Either that or no one was here. In this case, my mission would be nothing. Maybe it was a trap. However, I knew he was here. I could feel deep in my gut that he was here somewhere.

I cringed when the gate squeaked when I pushed it open, only wide enough for me to squeeze through. I glanced around, but all was silent, and no one was around to hear anything. All was still silent in the compound. Not even a window was open, nor was a curtain shifting to observe me. Despite all the noise I made upon entry. I should have been alert for a trap, but anger pushed those feelings aside. I carried on walking ever closer to the front door. When I was about twenty feet away. I stopped dead in my tracks when the front door swung open.

There in the doorway stood Torres laughing his head off. I grimaced at his laughter echoing around the empty, silent compound. "Hahaha, Brazen," he roared with laughter, holding onto his ample belly. "What do you want? How did you like the present I left you? Stupid of you to steal something that belonged to me. No matter how much I wanted her back. I changed my mind when I saw her. I didn't want any stolen, soiled second-hand cast-offs. Especially when she was full of your devil's spawn."

Here in front of me stood the man I desperately wanted to see. I was speechless with anger. I couldn't respond to his comments. All I wanted to do was wreak revenge on him for what he did to my wife and baby. It would take an eye for an eye to satisfy my hunger to bring him down. While at the same time, he was busy laughing at what he had done to me and my family. I slowly pulled my gun out from the back of my jeans. I pointed my gun at Torres and pulled the trigger. I got him right where I aimed. Gotcha when it landed right between the eyes...

The surprised look on his face when the bullet struck right between the eyes. He never knew what hit him. He landed on the ground in a cloud of dust. I'm sure he was dead before he even hit the ground.

Revenge was sweet. I had come to do what I had come to do. Before I knew what was happening, the windows were flung open, and a hail of bullets flew in my direction. I threw my arms open wide, ready to take them all. I smiled while simultaneously taking my punishment while they stole me away from this lifetime. I knew this was going to be my last day on this earth. I would no longer be in pain anymore. Now, I could be happy together with my wife and baby girl. I feel my body getting hit and flung every which way while falling to the ground. Now, I could finally be at peace and happy once again.

In the distance, I was sure I could hear the roar of bikes. Mo and the others must have guessed where I was headed. Now they could take me home with them. I could no longer feel any pain; nothing but peace and calm. I was slowly drifting off with the loss of my blood flowing in a pool around me in the dust. My story is over now as I leave this life to be with my one true love. Sorry, Mo, that I did this to you. I hope you will forgive me and understand one day.

Epilogue
Brazen

I smiled when I saw the beam of light beaming in my direction. Here she was, my sweet angel Christa. She had come to take me to be with her. She was holding my sweet, beautiful baby Delilah Rose in her arms. I knelt and grabbed her upper arms, running my thumbs up and down. "I've been so lost without you, my darling," staring her in the eyes, showing my deep love for her and seeing it beamed back to me. "I felt the pain of not having you by my side anymore. I've been waiting for you to come and carry me home. I wanted to be with you. I missed you so much. All my love left with you, and I had nothing left to give." I needed to justify to her why I was here with them now.

"I wish it wasn't so soon, my darling Brazen. You had a lot you still could have achieved in your lifetime, baby. Not that I'm sad to see you. Now that you're here. We can be with you together forever. I no longer need to keep wishing I wasn't there watching over you. While you lived out there alone in the real world." I tenderly brushed the hair over his eyes out of the way to stare him deep in the eyes once again. "I'm here, baby, and won't ever leave your side again."

"I feel such love and joy being back with you again, my darling baby and our gorgeous baby daughter. I love you, and I miss you so very much. I was sad I never met our baby girl. It was gutting me. I'll never be able to forgive myself for not being there when you needed me the most. Fuck it's making me angry that you were left alone to die in our house with no one to protect you. If I had any intel that he was after us, I would never have left that night."

"Sssshhh baby, it's okay. You're here now with us, and we will be together for eternity." I grabbed his hand and pulled him along. I passed Delilah to him to hold and love now that he was here. At the same time, we all walked together toward the light of our future.

****

Mo

"Fuck" I yelled when we got closer to Torres' compound. I could even hear the hail of bullets over the roar of our bikes. Brazen was going to be toast. No way would he survive that hail of bullets. Fucking idiot, why couldn't he say he was going and take us with him for backup? He sure had a death wish going on there. I wish I could have foreseen this and prevented this from happening to my best friend.

We pulled up to the compound gate and got off our bikes. We had our weapons drawn, ready, and prepared to fight back. My heart sank when I saw Brazen's body lying motionless in the dirt. There was no hope he would still be alive with the amount of blood surrounding his body. I spied another body in the distance near the front door.

It looked like Torres by the ample belly on the man. Brazen's final mission was successful, at least. He had managed to get in and kill his nemesis, too, meaning he was no longer walking this earth. I hope he was rotting in hell already. Sad that we had to lose Brazen's life in the process. We started firing back when Torres's men began firing in our direction.

"Listen," I called out, holding my arms up in the air and dropping my gun to the ground. This had to stop now. I was determined to call a truce to retrieve Brazen. "Hold your fire," I pleaded with Torres' men. I ordered my men to pull back and wait. They weren't happy but did as I asked of them. They dropped their weapons to the ground and raised their arms in the air. At the same time, I waited and hoped for Torres's men to stop firing and drop their weapons.

"We aren't here to get you. We don't have any beef with you nor wish to harm you. Let me in alone to come and get Brazen's body so we can take him home. We will leave you to do as you wish with your boss's body, too." I waited to see if they would respond. Nothing, only silence.

I took that as a sign of confirmation and decided to chance it and see what would happen should I open the gate to enter their compound. I sucked in a breath, inched forward, and opened the gate. I cringed when it squeaked while pulling it open. I stopped and waited to see whether his men would start anything again. I could see they still had their weapons trained on me, but relief set in when they weren't firing at me. Nothing, so I entered, keeping alert while I strolled in, walking over to Brazen's body on the ground.

I felt for a pulse to make sure. But as I expected, there was nothing. I swear the bastard was even smiling back at me. I made the sign of the cross as a mark of respect. I whispered to him, hoping he could hear me in the afterlife. "I hope you can hear me, you fucking bastard. I am pissed you went without telling me or anyone. I'm mad you didn't let us come with you for backup and help you out here. I know you're probably dancing up in heaven and being happy with your two babies again. I will miss you, my friend. Please wait for me until we meet again. God bless ya." I was damn glad Torres' men let us have this truce for now to retrieve our dead.

I grabbed him under the arms, lifted his body, and dragged him across the compound to where his men waited outside the gate. They lined up silently, their feelings hidden, but I felt their pain too. They saluted Brazen while I dragged his body past them and over to my bike. I draped his body over my bike with what dignity I could offer and hopped onto my seat, holding onto him with one arm. I started my engine and began the slow ride back to our compound. We all drove back slowly in a loud procession of bikes, mourning our lost leader. I could barely see the road at times when sorrow overtook me. I felt the tears run unheeded from my eyes. I angrily brushed them away, trying to think of our memorable times together over our lifetime as close friends and brothers.

I sighed with relief when we finally made it back to our compound. I cut the engine and swung my leg over to get off. I reached over and grabbed Brazen's body off my bike. I swung him into my arms, walked across the compound, and took him inside. I lay him on the sofa in the lounge room while I got my breath back. I told Anthony, who had followed me in, "call Doc. Tell him to come here ready to do the formalities for Brazen's death."

I stared down at his lifeless body. "Fuck, pal," I cursed at him again. "Why did you have to do this alone? I hope you're up there happy that you got Torres. I hope he's rotting in hell already. I'm sure you're happy with your lady and baby girl. Finally, together as one great, happy family again. Leaving us here to mourn for you and clean up your mess. Till we meet again, Pal." I turned away before I lost it again.

I needed to be strong for myself and the other men. I walked over to the bar, grabbed the bottle of whiskey, and took a swig. I needed to drown my sorrows. I hadn't touched a drop in years, thanks to my tumultuous past. I shouldn't do this. I didn't want to start that period of my life again. I didn't need to live in a dark, senseless pit under the stupor of alcohol. I took the bottle and threw it at the wall, watching it smash and the broken glass tinkle to the floor in tiny crystals and the whisky run like a river down the wall. I was angry at myself and angry at Brazen for being so foolish.

"You know that won't fix anything nor bring him back, Mo," Anthony piped up.

"Gah! I know! Fucking tell me about it. I should have known he would have gone and done something stupid like this. I should have kept a closer eye on him. I could see he was broken and wasn't coping. I should have done more to help him."

"Don't beat yourself up over it, pal. You're not his dad, and he was the prez. He could have overruled you and done what he wanted to anyway," I tried to tell him compassionately.

"Thanks." I glanced over at Anthony. I was very grateful he was with me. Everyone else seemed to have disappeared, probably back to their rooms or safe places. "Since I was the vice prez and, Brazen is now gone. With his position vacant means, I'm the new prez. Therefore, would you like to become my Vice Prez?"

"Wow, Mo. I'm speechless. It's a most unexpected honor. Thanks, Mo. Are you sure I'm up to the position?"

"Of course, I have the utmost faith in you. I'd trust you with my life, which is the most important thing. If you can't trust your vice president... It's yours. Not today, but I'll call the church tomorrow morning and make the announcement."

THE END

Other books by Scarlett Redd

Always – An Erotic Short Story

Luck of an Ice Badger – Erotic Short Story

Five Miles Out – Part One of The Liberty Belle Series

Savannah's Legacy – Standalone.

Broken Glass

Into The Shadows

Out Of The Shadows

Brazen

It's A Lonely World – Coming 2024

You can follow Scarlett on the following Social Media

Facebook https://www.facebook.com/scarlettredd2016/

Twitter @scarlettred1986

Instagram https://www.instagram.com/scarlettreddauthor/

About the Author

I am a writer of fictional contemporary dark romance. I work on both short stories and novels. I have a unique style of inserting twists in my stories giving them an unexpected spin to keep my readers on edge. I've always been an avid reader; I try to read as much as I can, which also helps polish my style of writing.

I currently live and work in Australia. When I'm not writing, I'm a busy mum to 3 kids and a couple of cats. I also share my wicked sense of humor, making my friends shake their heads since they're used to me. I also work as a Carer to special needs people when I'm not pursuing my other interests of reading and card making. I try to fit as many activities as I can into my already busy life. I also love traveling and finally getting to do a bit more now that my children are getting older. It also gives me the chance to annoy some more of my friends when visiting.